SO-AGE-967

NIGHT OF SHADOWS

Also by Edward Gorman

GRAVES' RETREAT

NIGHT OF SHADOWS

EDWARD GORMAN

A DOUBLE D WESTERN

Doubleday

NEW YORK LONDON TORONTO SYDNEY AUCKLAND

A DOUBLE D WESTERN
PUBLISHED BY DOUBLEDAY
a division of Bantam Doubleday Dell Publishing Group, Inc.
666 Fifth Avenue, New York, New York 10103

DOUBLE D, DOUBLEDAY, and the portrayal of the letters DD are
trademarks of Doubleday, a division of Bantam Doubleday Dell
Publishing Group, Inc.

Library of Congress Cataloging-in-Publication Data

Gorman, Edward.
Night of shadows/Edward Gorman.—1st ed.
p.   cm.—(A Double D western)
I. Title.
PS3557.O759N5   1990
813'.54—dc20   89-11955
CIP
ISBN 0-385-24561-0

*This is for Joe Lansdale,
one of my favorite people and
favorite writers*

This book is based on the fact that in the late 1890s a woman named Anna Placak became Cedar Rapids's first female uniformed police officer. She may well have been, according to several histories, the world's first female uniformed officer as well.

—EG

NIGHT OF SHADOWS

The cellar was a place of spiders and mice and shadows. It was also a place where Mother stored plump, colorful jars of the preserves she was so proud of—red for strawberry, blue for blueberry, yellow for peach. Mother often won prizes for her preserves at the county fair. Last year, 1894, she'd won first prize in two categories.

The cellar was also one other thing—his prison.

When the door creaked open above him, exposing an oblong glimpse of blue sky or midnight stars, he knew food was being brought to him, or the medicine Mother dispensed to keep him calm so he would not think about creating another "incident."

Sometimes, in certain moods, he agreed with Mother that the cellar was where he belonged, ankle-chained to the post in the northeast corner. His compliance with her wishes usually followed another "incident." She would feel he was "Oh thank God, all right again," and then she would let him up from the cellar, and then things would be fine again for a time and everybody in the prosperous neighborhood would say how good it was to see him again and ask him how his "trip" had been (Mother had convinced the neighbors that he was a sales representative, taking train rides to far and exotic points such as Dubuque and Des Moines and Peoria)—but then it always started to happen again and Mother started to sense it and so she'd take to following him (without his realizing it) and see that he was becoming "troubled" once more and focusing on a certain man or woman in the city.

And so back to the cellar he'd go.

He should never have told her about what he'd done. About the shallow grave west of the tracks east of the town. Or the one he'd thrown into the rapids downriver on a chilly March night two years earlier. Or the one—

And so, back to the cellar he'd go, waiting for oblong glimpses of blue sky or midnight stars, befriending once again the spiders and mice that he let crawl over his body to show them he meant no harm.

He liked it especially when it rained at night when, ankle-chained to the post, he could hear the rain thrumming on the slanted cellar door. He felt very snug and secure at these times and forgot entirely any desire for another "incident" to take place.

Oh, yes, at these times he forgot the incidents entirely and just gave himself up to the sweet smell of Mother's preserves and the damp, cool darkness of the cellar and his friends the spiders and the cute, chittering mice.

ONE

They were about the sort of prisoners you would expect to find in the Cedar Rapids jail on a May morning in 1895.

Anna Tolan walked up and down the long cellblock dispensing coffee, toast, and eggs. A few of the male prisoners—those whose hangovers hadn't blinded them—took obvious and fond note of Anna's pretty Irish face and slight but pleasant figure. Her blue eyes and faintly freckled face went well with her crisp light blue pinafore that she had starched and pressed herself. She might have been any other twenty-six-year-old woman except for the bold, silver police badge pinned to the right shoulder of her pinafore.

As usual in the morning, Anna had checked the logbook downstairs to see what sort of humanity she'd be dealing with in her job as matron. Nothing exceptional presented itself, the men all in here for drunk and disorderly, wife beating, driving horse and buggy while intoxicated, or bootlegging liquor.

Sometimes there were streetwalkers, counterfeiters, cocaine addicts, and men involved in white slavery. These sorts gave Anna more pleasure than the drunks because they provided for better conversation over dinner at the boardinghouse where she lived.

"You married?" asked a brazen yellow-haired young man in a plaid drummer's suit that had been torn up in a fight.

Even in his somewhat dazed condition, it was obvious the man could see the difference that came over Anna's face.

"No, I'm not," she said.

She felt her heart hammering, her face flushing, not out of embarrassment, but grief. A year and two months had passed, and she still had not been able to quite go on with her life. Every time somebody mentioned it—

She repeated herself more softly. "No, I'm not."

Then she moved on down the cellblock, bearing the wide

tray filled with breakfast, doing her best to be pleasant with men who were most likely frightened and ashamed. At least the decent ones would be frightened and ashamed.

In the last cell she found a prime example of a decent one. Scarcely a man, more likely a gangly boy who just happened to be tall as a man, he sat hunched on his cot, head down on his knees and crying softly. He was alone in the cell.

Anna said, "Breakfast will make you feel better."

He went on with his weeping.

Anna hesitated a moment before speaking again, looking out through the barred windows at the china blue spring sky. Below, Cedar Rapids sprawled out before her, an industrious city of nearly twenty thousand, with electricity, more than four hundred telephones, an opera house that featured the most famous theatrical acts in the world, and innumerable factories that were the envy of the state.

Anna watched as a horse-drawn trolley clanged its way down Third Avenue, people running to catch it as the day was just now beginning at 6:35 A.M.

Anna turned back to the boy. "Here. You'll feel better if you eat."

For the first time, he looked up at her. With his snub nose and tender mouth, he reminded her of her young brother Robert back on the farm in Parnell.

"I only got drunk 'cause Virginia said she wouldn't marry me," the boy said, wiping his nose on the back of his hand.

"Here," she said again.

"What'll the judge do to me?"

He was scared. She smiled. "Not much. Not if you tell him about Virginia and not if you tell him that you don't plan to do what you did ever again."

"I didn't mean to hit Curly."

"I'm sure you didn't."

"He just made some remark about Virginia."

"I understand."

He sort of laughed and he sort of cried in the way only a young man could. "Kind of funny, isn't it, me gettin' into a fight defending the honor of a woman who won't marry me?"

Suddenly he seemed to notice the food and the unmistakable look of hunger appeared in his brown eyes. "I'm going to throw myself on the mercy of the court," he said, reaching through the slot in the bars through which his food tray fit, "and tell the judge that I wasn't just defending the honor of Virginia—I was defending the honor of womankind everywhere." He paused and looked at her a moment out of the corner of his eyes, like a young kid waiting anxiously for approval. "How do you think he'll like that?"

Anna laughed. "If you can hold that expression you've got right now, he'll like it just fine."

Then she moved on to the last cell where two men as grizzled as the young kid had been innocent sat waiting to make a few dirty remarks.

After one particularly lewd suggestion, Anna said, "Isn't it a pleasure to deal with refined gentlemen?"

It was going to be a very typical day.

The Cedar Rapids constable's uniform consisted of a blue double-breasted jacket, matching trousers, black high-laced shoes, and a hat modeled on the French kepi. At this time of morning, you saw eight men in the official uniform, trailing into the meeting room now, hands filled with coffee cups and sweet rolls from a bakery three doors away. The station itself was three stories and had formerly been the Empire House, a hotel of some note back in the seventies.

Anna Tolan stood outside the meeting room, sipping on her own cup of coffee and greeting each officer who walked past her.

One, a chunky towhead with a handlebar mustache, said, "Why don't you marry me, Anna, and stay home and have us some kids?"

Anna poked him in the ribs and said, "And what exactly would you do with your wife, Olson?"

Olson grinned. "I'd figure out something."

The next man past her was named Peary, David Peary. He wore neither the double-breasted jacket nor the kepi. He was a detective, the only such bona fide creature in the entire town. He was tall with slick dark hair and dark eyes. He was, banker style, given to three-piece suits and the slender, board-room type of imported cigar. He was also, as all the women at the boardinghouse constantly reminded her, (a) very nice-looking in a somewhat cruel sort of way (it was his sharp aristocratic nose and thin line of lips) and (b) interested in taking her bicycling, an offer he'd made many times.

This morning, he paused next to her and said, "You're going to want to eavesdrop for sure this morning, Anna."

"Why?"

"Big news."

"What kind of big news?"

He smiled and touched her elbow. "If you'd gone bicycling with me last night, you'd already know."

And with that he walked into the big room with the west-facing window that had a desk, several chairs, and a big chalk-board sitting in the middle of the hardwood floor. The place smelled of furniture polish and cigarette smoke and apple blossoms from a tree down the block. A robin sat on a win-dowsill inquisitively watching the men.

Matrons were not, strictly speaking, constables. True, ma-trons carried badges. True, matrons had the power to arrest. True, matrons were summoned to impose law and order dur-ing times of emergency. But they rarely worked outside of the jail itself and even more rarely participated in the appre-hension of criminals. True, as Anna Tolan liked to remind everybody in the station house from Chief Ryan on down, there was a full-fledged policewoman in New York (she'd been assigned to the streets in 1888)—and therefore, as Anna gently suggested, there could well be one in Cedar Rapids ("Wouldn't that be some distinction?" Anna always said).

"Gonna be big this morning," Chief Ryan said, puffing past. "You'll want to hear this one."

"So I'm told."

Ryan, a wide six-footer with white hair and a handsome Irish face, said, "That, I take it, came from Peary."

She nodded.

"He'll do anything to get you to go bicycling, won't he?"

Anna felt herself flush—she did not like her personal life discussed here at the station—and Ryan, seeing his mistake, put a hand on her shoulder.

"I'm sorry, Anna."

"It's all right."

"I only meant to say that it's time."

"Maybe you're right."

"You're a good woman, Anna, and you're wasting precious years." He fixed her with grave blue eyes. "You've mourned enough. My Killarney grandfather used to say ''tis past mourning when the year comes round.' The year's come round, Anna."

He put his hand on her shoulder again and gave her a little encouraging shake and then went past her into the meeting room.

Twenty minutes later, concluding the first part of the meeting, Chief Ryan, his wide bottom perched on the edge of the desk, said, "I take you men are all familiar with a gunfighter named Stephen Fuller."

There was a general rumbling of recognition.

Chief Ryan said, "How many of you know that he was born right here in Cedar Rapids?"

This time there were no nods at all.

"Well, he was," Chief Ryan said. "Raised in an orphanage on the west side—till he ran away when he was thirteen." The chief paused then and looked to the back of the room. "Anna, why don't you just come in here and sit down?"

Anna smiled. She'd never been invited before.

She went in and took a chair. An apple blossom breeze came through the open window and the robin strutted down to the opposite end of the windowsill and Anna Tolan felt fine now, absolutely fine.

The other officers turned around and smiled at her—all but Detective David Peary who did not, for some reason, seem happy about her presence at all.

Chief Ryan said, "Fuller had a very good friend in the

orphanage. A man named Boyd Haskell who is a laborer at the Star Wagon Works over along the river. Boyd Haskell is dying of heart disease—I'm told he's in great pain—and the word I've had is that Stephen Fuller is coming in on a train today to see him."

"We gonna arrest him?" Murphy asked. He was young, red-haired, and freckled, and his exuberance was sometimes downright depressing.

"Nothing to arrest him for," Chief Ryan said.

"But he's a gunfighter."

"Was," Chief Ryan said. "Was a gunfighter. Those days are long gone. Wyatt Earp's getting to be an old man, Jesse James and Doc Holliday are dead, and most towns now have indoor plumbing. These days a gunfighter is about as useless an occupation as you can come by."

"So we're not gonna do nothin'?" Murphy persisted.

"We're going to stay calm is what we're going to do," Chief Ryan said. "And we're going to make sure that everybody else in Cedar Rapids stays calm. Hopefully, all we're dealing with here is one friend paying another friend a visit. He'll be here and gone before we know it."

"But you said he was a gunfighter," Murphy said.

"That's right. But he's not out of control. He's been a lawman in several towns, and served with a few judges over in Dakota Territory twice, and generally has only been known to draw when he's been goaded into it. Plus, he's forty-five years old and it isn't real likely that he's looking for any trouble. At least with anything but a bottle."

"He tip now and then?" Murphy grinned, showing the Irish love not only for drink itself but for tales about drink.

"As I get it, pretty seriously. In and out of hospitals, matter of fact," Chief Ryan said.

"You figure on meeting him at the train yourself?" another officer asked.

Chief Ryan nodded. "Yes, I do. And I also figure on being just as courteous and helpful as I can. I want him to see this Boyd Haskell and then I want him to go on his way. I telegraphed a marshal friend of mine in Kansas where Fuller has been living and I got his wire back this morning. He said that the only time Fuller would be a problem is when he's had a lot to drink and when somebody's been pushing him too hard." The chief surveyed the room. "I want you men to make sure that nobody *does* push him too hard. We've gone eighteen months without a killing in Cedar Rapids and I mean to keep things that way."

Murphy asked, "How're we going to stop it?"

"We're going to go to every drinking establishment in this town and tell the bartenders to keep an eye out for him and if he comes in there to make sure that none of their customers who like to fight start anything. I want you to let the bartenders know that we're holding them personally responsible for the behavior of their clientele and if they think I'm kidding, they're going to have a long time to think it over in Anamosa." Anamosa being, of course, the site of the nearest prison.

"Would you like any of us to accompany you to the station?" Detective David Peary asked.

"I appreciate the offer, David, but I think Mr. Fuller will feel more comfortable if I'm there alone. I don't want him to think we're challenging him or crowding him." He took out his briar pipe and put it between his teeth. "Anybody got any questions?"

From the back, Anna said, "Is it all right if I say something?"

"It sure is," Chief Ryan said.

"Maybe Mr. Fuller would feel better about being greeted by a woman."

The officer who had frowned at Anna earlier now rolled his eyes. Obviously he saw no place in a constabulary for a woman. Especially one who wanted to be deeply involved in critical constabulary activities.

Chief Ryan said, "You know something, Anna. That's a damn good idea. Pardon my French."

Anna then noticed David Peary. He looked no happier than the other disgruntled officer nearer the front. "No offense, Anna, but I think this Fuller would get the message that we expect him to be on his best behavior if the chief told him that himself."

Anna said, "Why do we have to tell him to be on his best behavior? Why don't we just say we're sorry his friend is dying and that we'll be glad to help in any way we can? That's what we'd do for anybody else who came to Cedar Rapids— why should we make him an exception?"

Now Anna noticed more frowns.

Murphy said, "Anna, maybe you don't know much about gunfighters."

"I grew up with three brothers and that was all they ever talked about. Jesse James and the Dalton Brothers and Billy the Kid. They're all I've ever heard." She paused. "All I'm saying is that if we're nice to him, we probably won't have any problems at all. He'll visit Boyd Haskell and get on the next train."

Chief Ryan said, "I think that's a damn good idea. Again, pardon my French, Anna. Let's just pretend that there's nothing special about him at all. We warn all the bartenders, we see that Fuller gets a nice room for the night, and in the morning he'll probably be gone, and we can get back to the business of getting ready for that damn county fair."

The county fair board tended to be an acrimonious group whose conflicting interests (part of the board wanted amusements for city folks, the other part wanted amusements for country folks, and the war never ceased) made its chairman— Chief Patrick Cletus Ryan—constantly take little bits out of his pipe stem with ceaselessly grinding teeth.

Chief Ryan turned to Anna. "Why don't you wait after the meeting here this morning, Anna, and we'll talk?"

Feeling David Peary's angry gaze on her, Anna flushed and bowed her head.

"Now let's talk about getting Shannon over at the livery to do something about his manure problem," Chief Ryan said. "Every woman who knows how to read and write has written me a letter about the smell and I want you to get on his back and stay on it. I want to see a honeywagon pulling in and out of there every four hours. Is that understood?"

All the constables knew enough to nod heartily. When Chief Ryan began getting letters about things left unattended or unresolved, he was not a man to disagree with.

The "manure problem" would be dealt with and dealt with today.

At the end of the meeting, Chief Ryan looked at his pipe stem. He'd taken two big chunks out of the end. Long ago he'd been wise enough to start carrying extra stems in his pocket.

"Now, he's not going to be a very pleasant fellow."

"I know that."

"He'll probably curse."

"Chief, I have three brothers. Cursing is not something I haven't heard before."

"He may even make a lewd suggestion."

"Chief, some of your own constables make lewd suggestions."

The chief paused and stared at her. He looked so odd at the moment, Anna couldn't guess what he must be thinking. "And he's a ladies' man."

"He is?"

"A notorious one."

"Oh."

"I've seen photographs of him. Very handsome devil. At least he used to be before John Barleycorn got ahold of him."

"I see."

"I just don't want you to get taken in."

She smiled and touched his arm affectionately. "Chief, I'm a grown woman. A widow. I'm not a silly young girl who's going to give her heart away to some gunfighter."

"Stranger things have happened," Chief Ryan said, which was what he always said whenever he started to lose an argument.

The apple blossom breeze came again and Anna closed her eyes and thought of her husband and how they'd gone walking six springs in a row along the Cedar and—

She felt unwanted tears in the corners of her eyes. "I don't think you have to worry about me, Chief. I don't think you have to worry about me at all."

Obviously seeing that she was thinking of her dead husband once more, the chief slid his arm around her and escorted her out of the meeting room. He pulled out his Waltham as he walked and said, "He'll be here on the three-oh-two." Then he laughed. "Which means the train should be pulling in about five."

Anna laughed too, thankful for the joke about the lateness of trains. It pulled her out of the sad mire of the past.

TWO

How they loved to hear it. How he loved to tell it. That it was untrue made it no less fascinating for either party.

They were on the Rock Island line in a mighty fancy bar car and Stephen Fuller had been drinking rye for two hours and talking for three.

"So you knew Wyatt Earp?"

"Yup."

"Knew him good?"

"Knew him very good."

"And the Reno brothers?"

"Spent six months with them."

"And Rube Barrow?"

"Showed him a few pointers with a Navy Colt."

"And Bill Doolin and Smoker Mankiller?"

"Tough boys, those."

"And Masterson? You really knew Masterson?"

"Knew him? Hell, son, I drew against him."

"You did?"

"Yup."

"Then how're you both still alive?"

And here the wink of the blue eyes and the nudge in the

elbow and the breaking white grin on the handsome sun-leathered face. "John Barleycorn. We were both so drunk we couldn't have hit the backside of an elephant if it'd had flags on it."

And the bar car—all twenty-three hayseeds who made up its passengers—roared with a roar seldom heard outside of circuses on the Fourth of July.

"And the Daltons?" someone else persisted tirelessly.

Quick sip of the rye and then a reflective pause that sort of put everyone on edge as the train swayed and bucked through the green midwestern day.

"The Daltons," Stephen Fuller said. "Now there was about the dumbest bunch of outlaws who ever put a bandanna across their faces." He shook his gray-streaked head, sending signals of derision to every attentive eye in the bar car. "Matter of fact, I can't recollect a dumber bunch of outlaws since the Younger brothers."

Awed voices. "The Younger brothers were dumb?"

"Son, the Younger brothers were so dumb they make President Harrison seem smart by comparison."

The laughter, if anything, was even louder now, the late President Harrison's agricultural policies having been unpopular in the plains states.

And so it went the rest of the trip.

Stephen Joseph Fuller (he'd always wanted a handle like Ringo or Wyatt or Sam, Stephen being the kind of name a mother liked) standing at the bar car, letting rube after rube buy him his next rye, a slender man of five-seven in a three-piece dark suit, a white percale shirt with a black string tie, a gray snap-brim fedora, a single and very earnest-looking Colt strapped across his waist, and a face that liquor had mottled but not destroyed. He still had—as he checked out each morning in the mirror—a classic profile and a way of making a classic profile seem perfectly natural. Men didn't think him pretty and women weren't alarmed by him—until it was too late.

Now, the air sweet with manure and spring soil from the

rich black earth on either side of the shining silver tracks, the talk turned to Pat Garrett and his killing of Billy the Kid.

"He really do it?" a drummer asked. "He really kill the Kid?"

Fuller sipped some more rye. "He did kill him indeed," he said in a voice worthy of a traveling Shakespearean. "But it broke his heart. It clean broke his heart."

Instead of a laugh this time, there was a sad sigh.

Pat Garrett's heart. Broken.

It was just terrible.

He always stayed too long. The one drink too many, the one story too wild for belief, and then they shrank from him, falling away as if he carried some terrible disease—which he did of course, that desperation that comes only from the bottle.

Two hours after his performance in the bar car, Fuller woke in a train seat across the aisle from an old lady with a colorful flowered hat, a black walking cane laid across her lap, and a glare of disapproval in her eyes that could have melted steel.

To her companion, a woman not unlike herself, she said, "They say he was a gunfighter. To me he's nothing more than a common drunk. Did you hear him swear?"

"I did," her companion said. "I most certainly did."

So it was the nightmare again, Fuller thought. He was never sure of what it was about, only that those who witnessed him in the throes of it always reported the same thing —how he writhed about, sweated, and swore. But when he awoke it was gone. He would spend the first ten waking minutes trying to puzzle it back together but—nothing. Nothing.

He reached for the bottle of water next to him on the coach seat. He was always smart enough to keep water close by because the dehydration was usually terrible. He took three long swigs, still aware of the two old ladies staring at him, and then he reached inside his suit pocket and pulled out the small calendar and pencil he kept there.

He put a black X across the date, May 6. On May 1, he'd noted down another X—the last day he'd taken any alcohol.

Which meant that he'd been able to go five days this time without a drink at all. Maybe other people would not think it worth bragging about, but Fuller did. If he could go five days . . .

He should never have gone to the bar car.

But in going back to the restroom he'd heard the laughter and smelled the tart elixirs being dispensed by the porter and then some part of himself over which he had scarce control took over and . . . then he was buying himself a drink and there were the tales of the James boys and Billy the Kid and—

Looking out the window now, wanting a bath and a clean change of clothes, a melancholy smile touched his lips. Even to himself he was foolish.

Wyatt Earp.

The Reno Brothers.

Doc Holliday.

He felt blood touch his cheeks and hoped that for the duration of the trip he wouldn't see any of the men with whom he'd been drinking, because as always there would be the smirks. Nothing more bold than smirks, of course, because for all his failings (drinks and his penchant for tall tales) he was still, after all, Stephen Fuller and he had in fact shot and killed twelve men in gun battles over the past twenty years— but smirks were enough. They pushed you into isolation and self-hatred as surely as a prison gate slamming shut.

He made, as always, two resolutions on the Rock Island headed for Cedar Rapids that afternoon when the daisies and bluebelles were blooming, when the cows on the hillside looked as immemorial as a Vermeer painting, when the first baseballs of the summer were being cracked into the outfield.

He resolved that he would never again have to put an X on the calendar he carried in his pocket.

And he resolved that he would never again tell tales of his exploits with famous gunfighters, not one of whom he'd ever laid eyes on.

At moments such as these he felt very good about himself as, once and for all, his problems had been sorted through, faced up to, and solved.

Yes, by God, he thought, tugging on his vest, sitting up straight, and glaring pridefully back at the two whispering old ladies; yes, by God, it was time he found pride in himself again and displayed it.

Then, right then, with the two old ladies still pointing at him and gossiping, he realized what the nightmare was always about.

The dank sights and smells of the orphanage returned in a rush that almost overwhelmed.

He had to turn abruptly away from the women and pretend to be looking out the window.

Tears filled his eyes and a deep and terrible shudder rocked his entire body.

The orphanage.

Of course.

The nightmare could have been about nothing else.

THREE

There was the oblong patch of blue sky. He thought back to when he was a boy. At this time of year he always took his kite to the hill up near the Bever property and watched the string stretch to the sun. One of his favorite stories in school had always been Icarus.

The oblong patch of blue sky—

He saw her long skirts and black shoes on the stairs. She was coming down.

She always walked a certain way when she was angry and she was angry now.

He moved back deeper into the cellar shadows, near the coalbin and the furnace.

Even so overweight, Mother was a handsome woman, one given to high-collared dresses and expensive brooches the size of a fist. She had steel-gray hair which she kept with the same pride his long-dead father had kept his chestnut mare.

She paused at the bottom of the stairs now, out of breath from exertion and anger. She had a newspaper in her hand, which she waved about like a prohibitionist waving an anti-alcohol pamphlet.

"I know you're here, James, and I want you to come out."

James said nothing.

"James."

Still nothing.

"James, you know that I don't have a strong heart. Do you want to be responsible for your mother keeling over and dying from a heart attack?"

That, of course, he could not resist. Responsible for your own mother's heart attack? How could you ever live with yourself? There would be a special place in hell for boys who caused their mothers to have heart attacks.

He came out of the shadows by the coalbin, into the long, wide patch of golden light cast by the sun through the open cellar door. Dust motes tumbled in the golden light. They were quite pretty.

She was much angrier than he'd imagined.

Usually when she saw him for the first time in a few days she was moved by the unshaven face and the dirty clothes.

But not today.

She thrust the paper in his face. "Do you recognize this, James?"

"It's a newspaper," he said.

"A Des Moines newspaper."

"Yes, Mother. I can see that it's a Des Moines newspaper."

"Well, look at the story on the front page in the left column."

He sighed. So she'd found out.

Dutifully, he took the paper from her and read it.

The story was simple enough, really. The body of a young man who'd been shot in the back was found in a shallow grave just outside the city limits of Des Moines. Local officials had discovered a curious metal disc that had been placed in the dead man's hand, a disc that was a piece used in a machine that mass-produced shoes.

Upstairs his mother had other papers—one from Illinois, one from Ohio, one from Missouri, one from South Dakota—that carried similar stories. The body of a young man found in a shallow grave. The disc from the shoe-making machine found in his hand.

She said, "Why do you do it?"

Now she sounded more exasperated than angry.

"They call me names."

"You think that's justification? You think that's justification?" *She was shrieking now.*

"I just get—those red flashes I've told you about. Those red flashes. It's not anything I can control, Mother. It really isn't."

She stared at him and then began shaking her head. "I don't know what to do anymore, James. I'd send you to California but—"

"I'd like California. I'd like it very much."

"But you'd get out there with Uncle Thomas and then one of those young men would call you names and then—then it would all come out." This time there was a certain pleading in her voice. "Don't you understand what they'd do to you if they ever found out?"

"Those men shouldn't have called me names. I can't help it how big I am."

Once more his mother shook her head. "People always call other people names, James. It's nothing to—"

He stepped over by her now. He was scarcely five-six but he weighed two hundred and fifty pounds. As usual when he hadn't shaved, there was an almost canine aspect to his face—the brown eyes and pink mouth—dog-like. Especially the eyes.

He said, "You baked today, didn't you?"

"What?" She'd been preoccupied, staring at the newspaper again.

"I said you baked today, didn't you?"

"Oh. Yes. Pumpkin pie."

"I could smell it. Down here."

"Oh."

"May I come up today and shave and take a bath?"

She sighed. "Do you think you've learned your lesson this time?"

"I'm going to do my best, Mother. I'm going to do my absolute best."

"I don't want you to go on the road again."

His eyes narrowed. "But what will they say at the office?"

"I'll fix it so you won't have to go. I still own half the stock. That will be no problem at all."

"But what will I do?"

"I'll ask Henry to find you some sort of office job."

He felt hollow inside. He loved putting on a new suit, one of the worsted ones he had made specially at Solomon Brothers, and taking his leather valise, getting on a Chicago and Northwestern train, and heading out to several cities on a sales swing for his father's shoe company. He liked the restaurants he got to dine in and he liked his furtive glimpses of beautiful young women and he liked being away from—

He always had a very difficult time admitting this: He liked being away from Mother.

Even given the relaxing rattle of the train.

Even given the shadowy elegance of the restaurants.

Even given the promising shapes of the young women.

Even given all these pleasures, no other pleasure was quite so great as—being away from Mother.

She touched his cheek now.

She was smiling for the first time today. "You're such a good little boy, James. I just get afraid for you is all. Afraid they'll find out and —" She shook her head resolutely. "If you're a good boy from now on, if you stay right here in Cedar Rapids, then I'm sure we won't have any trouble. I'm sure we won't have any trouble at all." Then she began to gush the way she gushed with her card-playing lady friends. "Wait till you see the plans I've made for your birthday next week. You just wait and see."

She always started planning for his birthday six months ahead of time. And she did make them very special days—no doubt about that.

Very special.

But he wasn't thinking about his birthday or special plans or anything like that at all.

He was thinking of how he was going to have to stay right here in Cedar Rapids.

No train trips.

No restaurants.

No glimpses of young ladies.

With Mother.

"Won't it be wonderful?" Mother said. "Aren't birthdays the most fun of all?"

"Yes," he said, knowing she wanted him to voice approval.

She kissed him on the plump cheek.

"I just can't believe it," she said. "My own little boy will be forty-two next week."

Half an hour later, he was upstairs shaving. He had already bathed. He wore a clean, white undershirt, white boxer shorts, and black elastic garters.

When she knocked on the door and said, "I've got a big piece of pumpkin pie for you downstairs. You hurry up now, you hear?" When she said this it grated on him.

He thought of never being able to leave Cedar Rapids again.

He thought of always being with Mother.

He looked down at the long, fine-boned straight razor in his hand.

"You hear me?" Mother called in her musical voice.

He looked at the pearl-handled straight razor. He wondered what it would look like slicing through Mother's throat.

"Yes, Mother," he replied. "Yes, I hear you."

FOUR

There was the man found dead drunk in the back of a buggy over by St. Luke's hospital. There was the old madwoman found wandering about without any clothes. There was the street woman arrested for prostitution and possession of cocaine. There was the man hauled away, protesting to the point of flying fists, on charges of operating a still. One man had struck his wife. One wife had struck a woman she suspected of taking undue pleasure with her husband. There was the eleven-year-old runaway found over by the Short Line railroad.

In other words, an unexceptional morning in the courtroom of Judge Horace B. Fenton, a robust man with muttonchops and a purple mole on his lower lip.

From the courtroom, those not permitted bail or who could not raise bail were escorted by Anna and a lumbering Swede trustee named Olson back to the jail, where Anna took the women and Olson the men to their respective cells.

By now the time was nearly noon and Anna knew that if she did not hurry, she would not have time during her lunch hour to get a present for Mrs. Goldman, the woman who ran the boardinghouse where Anna lived. Today Mrs. Goldman, sturdy and gentle Mrs. Goldman, was seventy-two years old, though you'd never know it by the certainty of her step or the pure beauty of her smile.

As Anna was leaving the jail, Chief Ryan came up. "You get any ideas where we can put up Fuller for the night?"

"Matter of fact, I did," Anna said.

"Where?"

"Mrs. Goldman's."

"Where you live?"

"Yes."

"Now why would you want to go and do a damn foolish thing like that? Pardon my French."

"You want to keep him out of trouble, don't you?"

"Yes but—"

"And you want somebody to keep an eye on him, don't you?"

"Well—"

"Then where's a better place than Mrs. Goldman's."

The chief started to protest but by that time Anna was already out in the warm spring sunlight on the pine boardwalk watching a cardinal perched on a nearby hitching post as she pulled her brand-new Imperial bicycle away from the side of the building. The Imperial was known to be the fastest model ever sold in Cedar Rapids and she certainly hoped so. She'd been paying two dollars a week on it to the Frank H. Drew Gun and Bicycle Shop on South Third Street for the past four months. When you only made ten dollars a week, that was a not inconsiderable sum.

Then she was off, feeling the wind on this apple blossom day, pumping the Imperial as if she were trying to impress the King of Siam himself.

Anna had a cousin in Parnell to whom she wrote every few weeks. It was Anna's intention to get the young woman, Margaret, to come to the city and join her, and so Anna made certain that her letters read like travel brochures, citing all the advantages to living in Cedar Rapids contrasted with a small farming community.

Anna regularly talked about how Mays Island was filled with beautiful picnic grounds and a roller coaster originally made in Italy and rivaling the "Whirlwind" in Chicago. She pointed out that Greene's Opera House regularly featured the most famous acts in the world, including Lillie Langtry. She noted that there were now more than seven hundred telephones in the city, one hundred and ninety-one electric streetlights, twenty-one miles of sanitary sewage pipe, and six miles of streetcar track running in each direction on all lines every twenty minutes. Now why would any sane twenty-two-year-old woman want to stay in Parnell?

Anna made her way down the dirt streets, passing infinite numbers and varieties of buggies, wagons, and coaches, and also passing what seemed to be infinite varieties of women in bustled dresses and outsized floral hats doing leisurely window shopping before such storefronts as Ludy & Taylor, Jewelers, Canfield's General Merchandise, and W. K. Taylor's Women's and Children's Furnishings. Over in what was known as the Kimball block, Anna went into Sands & Fellows, one of the best women's stores in the city, and bought a beautiful percale blouse set that would complement Mrs. Goldman's hair perfectly.

The brightly wrapped package stuffed under her arm, Anna got back on her Imperial and headed for the boardinghouse.

The thing she liked most about Mrs. Goldman's large three-story gray Victorian, with its widow's walk, cupolas, and turrets, was the way the elms surrounding the big corner property a few blocks off Fifth Avenue East formed a natural canopy over the east end of the property. At night you could hear the wind trapped in those lush leaves and it made a sound as sweet as music.

Mrs. Goldman, who never stopped working, was sweeping the front porch when Anna pulled her Imperial up to the steps.

"Good," said Mrs. Goldman when she saw Anna. "Now somebody can finish up that bean soup Mr. Tomlinson didn't eat."

She nodded to a skinny man in a funereal black business suit, with an exceptionally wrinkled face and a white billy goat beard, sitting in a chair reading a newspaper. He hadn't heard Mrs. Goldman's reference to him. He was ninety-eight years old.

"I'm not sure I'm going to have time to eat," Anna said, coming up the stairs.

For the first time, Mrs. Goldman stopped her sweeping and assessed Anna carefully. Mrs. Goldman, with her strong, appealing features, now looked concerned. "Nothing untoward happened at the station did it?"

That was one of Mrs. Goldman's favorite words, brought, she always liked to laugh, by her mother from Germany—"untoward."

"No, everything's fine at the station."

Once a man had hanged himself during the night and Anna had been the first official to see him. After work that day, she'd come back to Mrs. Goldman's, had gone up to her room, had thrown herself across the bed, said endless Hail Marys, and wept. Mrs. Goldman had brought in tea and sweet cakes and stayed up with her most of the night as Anna described again and again the man's face and how the flesh had turned ashen. Most especially how the eyes had bulged out.

"Good," said Mrs. Goldman with a nod of her gray head and rich dark eyes. She resumed sweeping at once. "Then you can go in and finish the bean soup. Be good for your bowels."

Mrs. Goldman was very big on talk about bowels, a fact Anna found both amusing and endearing, but now there were other subjects at hand.

"Mrs. Goldman," Anna said.

And the way she said it, Mrs. Goldman stopped sweeping again and looked up. "Something is wrong, isn't it?"

"No, it really isn't. But I do have to speak to you."

"I've never seen you like this, Anna. You're—different."

"I'm kind of in an—official capacity I guess you'd say."

"Oh, yes," Mrs. Goldman said, sounding perplexed. "I see. An official capacity."

"I have been asked by Chief Ryan to find lodging for a certain gentleman this evening. It will be for one night only."

Just then there was a breeze off the new spring grass and the new spring roses, and Anna had never smelled anything more seductive.

Down the front porch, the paper had fallen over Mr. Tomlinson's face. A violent snoring went on behind the sheets of newsprint.

"And this gentleman, who would he be?" Mrs. Goldman asked.

"His name is Stephen Fuller."

"I'm afraid I don't know who he is."

"Well, he's—a gunfighter."

"A man who shoots people?"

"Actually, I don't think he's shot anybody in a long time."

Mrs. Goldman laughed. "Well, good for him."

Anna smiled. "The chief is just afraid that once people find we've got a gunfighter in Cedar Rapids—well, there could be trouble."

"And what would bring such a man to such a peaceful city?"

"A friend of his lives here. The friend is dying."

"Oh." Mrs. Goldman was a woman of sorrow herself—her family's immigration had been marked with almost unceasing illness and accident—and now her eyes dropped and the edge left her voice. "You don't think this man will give us any trouble?"

"No, I don't think so. I'm going to have a stern talk with him."

Now Mrs. Goldman smiled again. "A slip of a girl like you —a stern talk with a gunfighter?" She put her hand on Anna's shoulder. "You're a good girl, Anna, and I know this must mean something to you or you wouldn't ask me about it."

A jay cried happily; Mr. Tomlinson snored.

Anna said, "They call me a constable, Mrs. Goldman, but what I really am is a matron. If I can get this Fuller in and out of Cedar Rapids without any trouble, I think they'll start looking at me in a different way."

"Men," Mrs. Goldman said with a certain air of disdain. "If they weren't so handsome and didn't have such fine strong voices, why would we even pay any attention to them?" She poised the broom to begin sweeping again. "He'll be here tonight?"

"Around suppertime, I suppose."

"Well, then, I'll make sure to have a very nice supper."

"Thank you, Mrs. Goldman. Thank you so much." Anna leaned over to kiss the woman on the cheek, and as she did so brought forth the gift-wrapped box. "And happy birthday, Mrs. Goldman."

Mrs. Goldman's eyes ignited with pleasure. "Why Anna, I—"

Anna giggled. "But remember, wait till tonight to open it. And no fair peeking."

Anna took her Ingraham from the folds of her skirt and looked at it. "Afraid you'll have to wake up Mr. Tomlinson and have him finish that bean soup."

Mrs. Goldman, hugging the package to her, said, "Now you get in there, Anna Tolan, and eat that soup. Your stomach needs it and your bowels need it. It won't take you more than three minutes."

Anna, laughing, knew a command when she heard one.

She slipped inside the cool shadows of the huge house and ate her bean soup in the big sunny kitchen. A chunky orange tomcat sat on the table watching her. His name was Toby and he was one of Anna's best friends. She blew on a spoonful of bean soup and then put it on a small plate for Toby and watched him eat. Toby ate everything. Five minutes later Anna was on her bright blue Imperial and headed back to work. Mr. Tomlinson was still snoring.

FIVE

He came in on the Rock Island, traveling coach, at 2:01 that afternoon. His name was Wendell George Parsons. He stood five-nine, was slender but not slight, wore bifocals, store-bought teeth and the black suit and Roman collar of an Episcopalian minister. He carried a *Chicago Tribune* in his left hand and a carpetbag of almost lurid color in his right.

As the other passengers swirled past him toward the depot, the good Reverend Parsons stood on the platform getting his first good look at Cedar Rapids. It certainly made a good first impression—the number of three-story buildings totaling at least two dozen, the wide streets kept clean despite the lumbering traffic of horse-drawn vehicles, the people dressed neatly in good middle-class clothes.

Yes, indeed, Cedar Rapids was a more than decent town.

Setting his bag down, he opened the *Tribune* to a page whose dominant headline read:

KILLER OF SEVENTEEN-YEAR-OLD BOY
STILL SOUGHT BY ILLINOIS AUTHORITIES

The story disclosed that the body of one Bernard Malloy had been discovered in a "shallow grave on the outskirts of Elgin," and that authorities throughout the state were on the lookout for the killer.

A smile touched the thin lips of the good Reverend Parsons.

What a help he could be—at least if he so desired—to the Illinois authorities.

Because he knew exactly who the killer was.

And exactly where the killer went.

That was why the good reverend had come to Cedar Rapids.

The smile remained on his face for a young mother pushing her infant in a fancy baby carriage with a fringed umbrella on top and beautiful, clean, blue corduroy inside. He then tipped his hat, picked up his carpetbag, and proceeded along First Avenue.

He knew that the letter would most likely have arrived by today and that a simple phone call would set in motion his plan to make himself wealthier than he'd ever been—even in the days before his reverend persona when he'd been a middling good cardsharp plucking rubes the way slaughterhouse workers plucked chickens.

The good Reverend Parsons, contemplating the impending upturn in his fortunes, began to whistle. The song was "Beautiful Dreamer," his favorite.

She read the letter quite carefully and without any emotion at all. She read it three times, and with fixated care. She tried to imagine what sort of man would write a letter such as this. Here in the vast living room with its Louis XIV furnishings and its Vermeer lithographs and the grand Steinway sitting on the tiles by the gigantic fieldstone fireplace—she could not imagine such a man at all.

She was seventy-three years old, a plump woman in a blue organdy dress with frilled high collar and massive brooches, a woman who had been a true beauty in her younger days, with a smile that ignited the marital hopes of at least two dozen suitors, a face flawless in its somewhat icy beauty, with ankles and wrists that had inspired a local man much taken by the poetry of John Keats to call her "a sylphan dream." Her father had owned the largest tannery outside Kansas City and her debutante party had attracted people from as far away as Zurich (her parents had traveled the continent incessantly, searching for something they did not find before heart disease took her father and influenza her mother), and at the late age of twenty-six, she, Susan Irene Bennecker, was given in matrimony to a rich shoe manufacturer named Clinton Hapgood Eyles, a stout man who spent some of his time with his golden Arabian horses, some of his time with his golden mistress

(Susan Irene Eyles one day decided to follow her husband, just to see what the woman looked like and was startled to realize that though she considered the girl ill-born, Susan Irene did have to concede the creature her unquestionable beauty), and some of his time trying to be a more forceful presence in the Iowa Republican party (Clinton had fallen on his mouth as a boy and now spoke with something of a vague lisp, which his political cronies saw as a definite impediment to succeeding in any meaningful way in their party). What remained of his time—he was older than Susan Irene by twenty years and as a consequence most of his work was done by his younger cousin who'd recently been made vice president—he spent with his wife and son. He loved them, there was no doubt about that, home life being a blizzard of gifts and compliments (all spoken in his lisp) and hugs (he was a very physical man). Then one gray November day, sitting in his office going over the monthly financial statement with his cousin, he fell dead of a heart attack.

What Susan Irene recalled of the mourning period was that there had been no mourning period. She had long realized that she did not love her husband, but not until he died did she understand that she had, in fact, despised him—his silly lisp, his silly horses, his silly political friends (in front of whom he was always groveling, never quite a man in their eyes because of his lisp), and his silly shopgirl mistress. In the twenty-four hours following his death, Susan Irene Eyles did three other things: She fired the Mexican maid she'd suspected her husband of sleeping with from time to time; told one of the more onerous of his cronies (a man with a mole on the tip of his bulbous nose) that she considered him vulgar beyond endurance (you could get away with such outbursts at such a time, the clucking family friends putting it down to the hysteria of the moment); and went into her husband's den and threw into the fire every one of the French postcards he had kept in the bottom left drawer of his massive oak desk.

They buried him on a raw day when the shovels had difficulty penetrating the dead, frosted earth.

And from then on things were quite different, quite different, in the Eyles household. Susan Irene had an abundance of money and could do exactly what she wished—and that was exactly what she did, most particularly with young James Hapgood Eyles.

Clinton, ever fearful that he would be thought less a man if his son were not the masculine ideal, had forced the plump and secretive seven-year-old into such sports as baseball, football, and wrestling (the latter a ritual Susan Irene found especially repulsive, putting her in mind of the homosexual Greeks she'd once read about), but that, of course, ended abruptly. Without Clinton's ravings to answer to, Susan Irene enrolled young James in piano lessons, hired a tutor to teach him the classics, and began taking him on long trips to Europe (much in the fashion of her parents) where James learned of painting and classical music and how one spent one's life well while appearing to do nothing much at all. Susan Irene was aware that back in Cedar Rapids her undue influence on young James was a matter of scorn and derision. He was inevitably called a sissy and herself called domineering (there was in the early 1890s a popular magazine concern about the "impulse to matriarchy" that was making young American boys a woefully inferior breed). But she did not care. She wanted a companion and she had the opportunity, with her son, to shape exactly the sort of companion she wished.

Not that young James complied so easily with all this. An obese boy (much as Susan Irene herself became obese shortly after the death of her husband), he spent his teen years trying to pull himself away from his mother's influence. Once he ran away to the neighboring hamlet of Hiawatha; another time he set fire to their stable; and on his seventeenth birthday she found him upstairs cutting open the breast of a wren whose skull he had earlier crushed with one of his mammoth fists). She sent him to see doctors, priests, and ministers of all sorts in order to get him to "become my sweet boy" but not until one night during his twenty-second year did she see him become the companion she had so long sought.

This had been after one of his first trips as a sales representative of his father's firm (the word "drummer" was as vile to her as the word "whore"). Late that spring night she crept up to his room to see why he'd been so insistent about going directly upstairs before even kissing her properly or asking her how her "social" had gone in his absence.

She had had a special door installed on his room, one with an exceptionally wide keyhole, so that she could kneel down and peer inside and see exactly what was going on.

And she had, shocked, seen the most unimaginable thing of all—James opening his leather valise and extracting from inside a bloody shirt far too small to be his own and a gigantic silver pistol which she recognized instantly as the one that had belonged to her husband.

Unable to stop herself, she got to her feet, burst into his room and began shrieking "What is going on here, James? What is going on?"

And so, beginning to sob, he sank to the edge of his bed, across from the bureau on top of which sat the photograph of his mother in one of the primmest of her collars, and told her what had happened in Indiana.

How he had not meant it to happen. How he could still not quite believe that it had in fact happened. How he had bought a pint of liquor and stayed in his hotel room for two days trying to pretend that it had not happened.

Then both sets of eyes fell on the bloody shirt strewn now like a wound on the white surface of the bed.

He fell to sobbing so violently that he seemed about to choke.

Then she sank next to him on the edge of the bed and took him in her arms and let him cry until he was completely spent, until all she had to do was ease him back on the plump mattress and let him fall into the most exhausted of slumbers.

From then on—both because she alone knew his secret and because she alone could comfort and succor him—she became not only his best friend, but his only friend.

The companion she had so long sought was hers at last.

"I want you to tell me about Illinois."

"What?"

"About Illinois."

He was having a snack of milk and cookies gnarled with fat brown chocolate chips. He sat at the kitchen table getting crumbs all over his shirt and all over the table. Ordinarily such a sight would have brought a smile to her face. She loved it when he did little boy things such as getting crumbs all over his shirt front. But things had changed since the arrival of the letter. Things had changed a great deal.

She said, there in the sunlight, the air rich with the smell of the freshly baked cookies, "I want you to tell me about Illinois."

"What about it?"

She held up the letter. "Something has happened."

He looked at the letter, his brown eyes curious, his pink mouth showing tiny tics of concern. "Who is the letter from, Mother?"

"I'm not sure."

"You're not sure?"

She paused. "Apparently it's from someone who knew you in Illinois."

"But I don't know anyone in Illinois. Except for Mr. Bainbridge. He's the wholesaler I call on in Elgin."

"There must be somebody else."

"There isn't."

"You didn't have any—companions when you were there."

"I don't have 'companions' anywhere, Mother."

She paused. "I've asked you not to take that tone with me."

"And I've asked you not to put me in the cellar."

"I hardly have any choice. Not when—" She paused. "Not when you've been a bad boy again."

"I'm not a bad boy, Mother. I haven't been a boy for decades."

She smiled. "Of course you're a boy, James. And you always will be." She forgot the letter a moment. "Look at the milk on your mouth and the crumbs on your shirt."

He flushed, brushing crumbs away with the displeasure one would visit on mites. "Who is the letter from?"

"You're getting strong again."

"What?"

"You take your trips and then—things happen. And then you come back to me and you're very weak and I must put you in the cellar and then you're the sweetest companion I've ever had. But after a few days—" She sighed. "After a few days, you get strong again."

There had been a time when she'd tried to keep him from taking the trips. For one, given the "flashes" he suffered, she was afraid that he would someday be caught and killed. But, also, once he got past the remorse for what he'd done, he grew strong—strong and cold and resistant, the way his father had been in the most secret part of his heart. Then James was no fit companion for her at all, and she found such periods in their lives almost unendurable.

He said, "I want you to tell me about the letter, Mother."

"It is from a man in Illinois."

"What man in Illinois?"

"He doesn't give his name."

"What does he say?"

She cleared her throat slightly. "He says he knows what you did outside of Elgin. He said he saw the man you killed and where you buried the body and that unless we give him five thousand dollars in cash, he will lead authorities to the body and will identify you as the killer."

She could see him become frightened. He was losing his strength. She wanted him to lose his strength, that vague air of cockiness.

"My God," he said.

"You didn't tell me about Elgin."

"I told you about Rock Island, though."

"Rock Island is not Elgin."

"It was just something that happened. I had the flashes again. I was afraid that if I told you—" He set his eyes to the crisp linen tablecloth. He brushed at more crumbs.

"You were afraid of what?"

"I was afraid you wouldn't let me take any more trips."

"I need you to tell me what happened in Elgin. Otherwise I won't be able to deal with this man."

"Do you think he'll really go to the authorities?"

But she was adamant. "I need you to tell me what happened in Elgin."

He stared across the table at her miserably. "He was just a man I met in a tavern not very far from the train depot. We started talking and then he got very drunk and started whispering things about me to another man down the bar. I—I just had another one of those flashes, Mother. I couldn't help myself. I waited outside for him. I followed all the way back to where he lived by this small stream and—" He shrugged. He was beginning to cry.

James was forty-one and dressed in a fancy white percale bosom shirt—and still he looked like nothing so much as an overfed six-year-old. She relished it when he looked like this.

"So you have no idea who might have written this letter?"

"No."

"You're absolutely sure?"

He was crying now with a certain vicious dispatch. "I'm absolutely sure, Mother."

She glared at the letter as if it were the direst of enemies. She could not recall ever feeling quite so despondent as she did at this moment.

"You won't let him go to the authorities, will you, Mother?" James sobbed.

She laughed softly and stood up and went around the table and leaned over him and put his face deep into her bosom.

She kissed him with wet expertise on the cheek and then just at the edge of the mouth and said, "Now do you know why it's so important to be the good little boy I want you to be?"

"Oh, yes, Mother," he cried. "Oh, yes, Mother, now I understand. I really do!"

SIX

On the depot platform were two reporters, a burly constable dressed up in a suit that fit him twenty pounds ago (Chief Ryan decided to send some help for Anna even if she didn't want it), and idlers of assorted types—from beer-breathed "authorities" on gunfighters, to pool hall loungers who didn't believe that anybody like Stephen Fuller was actually coming to a burg such as Cedar Rapids, to at least a dozen boys with cowlicks and excited grins. O'Malley, a policeman, had dropped the word ("though you'll have to keep this to yourself") to Smcjek the baker who in turn dropped it to Finestein the tailor who in turn had dropped it to Mrs. Getz his customer who in turn . . . And so, by two o'clock that afternoon, up and down the city streets, from the lazy chatter of the cabbies sitting in their horse-drawn carriages waiting for fares to the eager whispers of the students at the Cedar Rapids Business College, the word went out. Stephen Fuller, a man who had shot twelve others (though there were some, by three o'clock, who put the number at more than twenty) would be standing right here on the platform of the depot as soon as the train could deposit him.

There was a peculiarly festive air surrounding the depot, as if what was pulling in was one of those large circus trains that came here once a year. The sun seemed a little hotter now, the sky a deeper blue, and the ragged clouds an almost impossible white.

Anna, in her blue and white pinafore and her constable's badge, stood on the edge of the platform trying to look comfortable with all the commotion about her. She knew how important it was to handle this situation easily and without problems.

Ferguson, the chunky cop in the too-small suit and the

heavy doses of bay rum cologne applied to his cheeks, came over and said, "Chief told me to tell you I'll be right behind you with my hand on my Colt."

She looked at him and frowned. "What do you think he's going to do, Ferguson, shoot me?"

"With this kind you can never tell."

He tried hard to sound sage, but he couldn't convince her of his wisdom because, like her, he was only a few years off the farm and the only time he'd ever encountered a gun-fighter had been in the pages of the *Police Gazette.*

She turned away from him as somebody shouted, "Here it comes!"

And indeed it did, a wood-burning locomotive pulling maybe nine passenger cars, and headed with great smoke and fury to the platform on which they waited.

Ferguson tapped her on the shoulder. "Remember what I said, Miss Anna." He then patted the Colt he was carrying in a shoulder holster inside his jacket. Beneath his derby, he offered her a ludicrous wink. He looked both so earnest and so foolish that she had to grin at him. It was sweet of him to want to protect her but he was about as ham-handed and melodramatic as one could be.

Then the train was there, smelling of fire and oil and heat, still a miracle to Anna, its speed and strength and the places it spoke of—Denver and Cheyenne, San Francisco and San Diego, lands as exotic as China when she'd never once been out of Iowa (well, except for a church trip once to Moline, Illinois, across the Mississippi).

Then he was there too, and he was both much less impressive (she saw immediately that he suffered the pallor and the stooped posture of the drunkard) and more impressive (there was about him an air of melancholy that moved her at once, and in that melancholy was a hint of rage and danger), a tall and slender man in a dusty blue three-piece suit and a gray snap-brimmed fedora worn at an angle that would have been more rakish if his hair weren't now mostly gray, the rakish angle hinting at the sad last vestige of his pride and vanity.

He stood squinting in the sun as the waiting crowd pushed

its way through the other passengers who'd gotten off with him. The boys called out his name in tones both reverent and frightened; the reporters, pads and pencils poised, shouted a few questions at him; the pool hall idlers snickered, obviously feeling that their cynicism had been justified, Fuller being nothing more than a worn-out forty-year-old. Ferguson looked at Anna once more, winked again, and patted his Colt.

This time, mischievously, she winked back. She was glad to see that she'd made him blush.

She gave them a few more minutes, the boys and reporters and sneering pool hall punks, and then she moved in decisively, keeping her badge evident on the breast of her pinafore.

She got him by a frail elbow and said, "Mr. Fuller?"

He glanced down at her and she saw in that instant that all the stories were true, at least those pertaining to his enthusiasm as a ladies' man. Where a moment before her appearance his coloring had been ashen and his expression disinterested, his face now exploded with interest and a sly winsomeness. He aimed himself at her like a weapon.

He tipped his hat and said, in a voice resonant and well modulated through long practice, "Hello there, miss."

"I'm Anna Tolan. I'm with the Cedar Rapids Constabulary."

He nodded to her badge. "I don't believe I've ever heard of a female police officer before."

The reporters were still asking questions; the boys jostling to get close to him.

"I'd like to help you find some lodgings."

"Well, I'd appreciate that, ma'am."

"Then why don't you follow me?"

"Be my pleasure." Again there was a hint of the flirt in his words and the new life in his blue gaze.

A reporter said, "When was your last gunfight, Mr. Fuller?"

She watched his face for reaction. He tensed up, no doubt about that, and pain narrowed his eyes. "That's a closed subject, as far as I'm concerned. I'm no fighter anymore." He looked at Anna and smiled. "These days I'm just a lover." She might have been insulted by his boldness except that he looked close to tears. Her eyes dropped to his slender hands —really, the graceful hands you might expect to find on a well-bred gentleman instead of a gunfighter—and she saw how those hands trembled. So the stories about his drinking hadn't been exaggerated after all. She thought of her own father back on the farm and how one day, because he was usually drunk by the time he'd finished chores in the morning, he'd been crushed by a bull whose charge he might have escaped if he'd been sober.

Taking Fuller's elbow again, she said, "Come on. My bicycle's over there."

He gave a would-be jaunty little salute to the gathering of onlookers and then let her lead him away.

"I'm not the attraction I used to be," he said five minutes later.

"I beg your pardon."

"In the old days that platform would have been overflowing with people come to see me."

"Really?"

"Absolutely. A tent-show man from back East wanted to send me on tour."

"That must have made you proud."

"I take it you don't much like me."

"You've made a reputation killing people, Mr. Fuller. Is that something you're proud of?"

"It was different in the old days. On the frontier. I'd been a lawman for a time and then I went to work as a security man and they were just the sort of jobs where killing sometimes happens."

"I see."

"You don't believe me?"

"I don't know yet, Mr. Fuller, if I believe you or not."

He smiled and nodded to her Imperial. "That's a beauty."

She was happy to change the subject. They were moving up First Avenue, walking near the trolley tracks. Women in big picture hats glanced at the dissolute but handsome man who kept stride as Anna slowly pedaled her Imperial. There were kids with balloons and kids with ball bats and kids with big paper cups of strawberry refreshment. School was out and the apple blossom breeze and the beautiful orange monarch butterflies riding it seemed to lead the kids to certain wonderful and mysterious places.

"Nice town," he said.

"Are you being sarcastic?"

"Not at all. Why would I be sarcastic?"

She lost balance on the Imperial a moment and he had to grab her. As his surprisingly strong hands took her, she felt herself flush and become uncomfortable.

Once she was righted again, he let go of her. He walked through the late spring afternoon.

"Now, why would I be sarcastic?"

"Oh, just the way people are."

"What people?"

"Big-city people, I guess."

"What about big-city people?"

"Well, some of them consider Cedar Rapids to be sort of a hick town."

He gestured grandly to the electric light and telephone poles. "How long have you had electricity?"

She shrugged. "Ten years I guess."

"And how many phones are there here?"

She could not keep the pride from her voice. "More than four hundred."

"Do you know there are parts of Chicago without lights *or* telephones?"

"Really?"

"Really. So Cedar Rapids is hardly a hick town."

She looked at him then and for the first time she let a certain fondness for the man she'd been trying to wrestle down inside herself show in her eyes. "Really," she said. "Is that true? About certain parts of Chicago?"

"Really," he said, and she could see a certain fondness in

his eyes, too. "That's really true about certain parts of Chicago."

No fuss was made at Mrs. Goldman's.

Mr. Tomlinson with his billy goat beard still slept on the front porch and the other boarders—the German railroad man, Krauzer, waiting for reassignment from the Rock Island, and the drummer, Nosbish, home for a day before once again "assaulting the wilds" as he always put it, and Miss Dailey the schoolteacher—all nodded to Fuller as Mrs. Goldman led him along the upstairs hall to his room, but there was no untoward staring and certainly no untoward remarks.

Fuller put down his carpetbag on the bed, glanced around the room and then sniffed. "Incense?" he said to Mrs. Goldman.

"I hope you like it."

"Very nice smell."

"Sandalwood. It's my favorite," Mrs. Goldman said. "I burn a little in each room every day. My boarders seem to enjoy it."

He took off his hat and tossed it, not without ceremony, on the bed, next to his carpetbag. Then he drew in a deep breath and looked around again and then he looked once more at Anna and said, "You going to go over with me when I see Boyd Haskell?"

"I thought I might."

He smiled at Mrs. Goldman. "This pretty young woman here is convinced that I'm going to shoot somebody if I ever get out of her sight."

Anna started to protest but Fuller turned the moment into a joke. "I take it you'll let me take a bath alone?"

Anna laughed. "That's something I won't bother with at all."

"You want some hot water?" Mrs. Goldman said.

"I sure would appreciate it," he said.

Mrs. Goldman nodded and left.

He said, "She always this nice?"

"Always."

"And you—are you always this nervous?"

She felt herself flushing again. "I'm a constable, Mr. Fuller. I'm doing my job."

He startled her then by clamping down on his jaws and filling his eyes with anger. "The last time I killed a man was nine years ago and the only reason I did it was because he was trying to backshoot me. Now how about treating me like something other than a rabid animal?"

"I didn't think I was treating you that way."

"It's in your voice. It's in everybody's voice."

"I'm sorry, then, Mr. Fuller. I didn't intend to sound that way at all."

"And will you please for God's sake quit me calling me Mr. Fuller? You make me feel like I'm your grandfather."

"Oh, you don't remind me of my grandfather at all." She smiled blandly at him. *"He* was a gentleman."

Then she turned, left the incense-fragrant room, and went downstairs to have some tea with Mrs. Goldman and watch the wrens peck for worms on the backyard grass.

SEVEN

In the lobby of his hotel, the good Reverend Parsons found a phone and several sheets of paper listing all the numbers in Cedar Rapids. Most of the numbers belonged to such businesses as the L. A. Bradley Stockyards, the Star Wagon Works, and the BCR&N Railroad office. But there were residences, one of which belonged to a Mrs. Eyles, and Reverend Parsons had no doubt that this was the number he sought.

The phone was on the wall in a dusty corner around which were piled boxes obviously meant to be trucked away. Through a dusty rear window Parsons could see the Cedar River and across it a long row of icehouses lining the opposite shore.

He lifted the receiver, cranked the phone and asked for the operator for number 523.

The odd thing, he thought as he waited for someone on the other end to answer, was that he felt no fear.

Back in Chicago he'd once been involved in a late-night burglary and he had discovered just how cowardly he was after all. He'd vomited before and after. His fellows had laughed at him. He'd fled Chicago for St. Louis where he remained for many months without ever quite calming down.

But this was different and he wondered why. Perhaps it was as simple as this: the Eyleses would never go to the police. Ever. Because if they did James Eyles would be arrested and eventually executed. That simple.

From the front came the industrious *clack* of a telegraph, a sound he'd always found fascinating.

Then a voice said, "Hello."

It was a male voice. It sounded muzzy and weary and morose. James, of course.

"Hello, James."

"Hello."

"Do you know who this is?"

Pause. "No."

"Can you guess?"

Another pause. "No."

"I'm the man who wrote your mother the letter."

"You."

"Yes."

A third pause. "I'm going to get my mother."

"I followed you that night, James."

"What night?"

"You know what night."

Silence.

"And then, James, I got into your hotel room and I went through your valise and I found all those newspaper clippings. You should never have clipped all those things from newspapers, James. Do you know why?"

"Why?"

"Because now I know that the man in Elgin wasn't the only one. There've been a lot of them, haven't there?"

Silence.

"There were even two of them right here in Cedar Rapids, weren't there, James? You had two clippings about hobos vanishing from the tramp jungle down by the tracks. And we know what happened to them, don't we, James?"

"I'm going to get my mother."

The receiver on the opposite end banged against the wall as James apparently let it dangle.

Reverend Parsons looked around the rear of the hotel again, out the dusty window. On the river now he saw a rowboat with a young couple in it. The man rowed mightily. The woman, tucked into the stern of the boat, sat beneath a bright pink parasol. Her head was thrown back in laughter. It was the perfect image for an afternoon well into the seventies and the sky a faultless blue.

"Hello," said a female voice, one that was all the things the male voice had not been. Stern. Confident. Threatening.

"I was just talking to James, Mrs. Eyles."

"You've upset him terribly."

"I'm very sorry."

"There'll be no—"

"Please, this is a party line, Mrs. Eyles, and I made a point with James to discuss nothing specific. I just meant to call and say that I'd be at your place in a half hour or so."

"But—"

"We need to sit down and have a nice civilized chat, Mrs. Eyles. I'm sure you have a lovely home and I'm sure that I'd enjoy myself—sitting on the veranda, perhaps, and sipping a whiskey and soda. That's a hint, in case you didn't guess, Mrs. Eyles. I like whiskey and soda very much."

"There'll be no whiskey and soda, whoever you are."

Reverend Parsons said, "There's no reason for your tone, Mrs. Eyles. This is a simple business deal. I feel no recrimination against James, and you should feel none against me."

Mrs. Eyles did just what he'd been expecting her to do. She hung up.

"I think it's a stupid idea."

"I don't recall asking you your opinion."

"Well, I'm giving it."

"He seems nice enough."

"I'm told Jesse James was a charmer with the ladies, too." David Peary put his hand on her elbow so he could stop her from continuing to file. They were in one of the tiny back offices of the police station. He'd followed her in here, obviously angry. "I hate to say it, Anna, but I don't think you know what you're doing."

"Chief Ryan seems to think so."

David Peary obviously had to choose his words carefully. It would not be fitting for a detective—especially one who stood on formality as much as Peary did—to speak up against his own chief. "The chief—"

She teased him a bit. "The chief what? What were you going to say, David?" Another of the matron's duties was to file in the big wooden cabinets all the paperwork done in a given day. Anna, who was no demon of organization herself (men always assumed women were organized, an occasionally dangerous notion), liked this part of her job least.

"Well, the chief likes you. You're like his daughter. So when you came up with this silly idea of yours—"

She stopped him right there.

No doubting his competence as a detective. No doubting his handsomeness. No doubting his romantic interest in her. And, to be honest with herself, no doubting her own occasional romantic interest in him. But calling her idea "silly . . ."

She was angry and then she was hurt and then she was angry again and then she was hurt again. All this took less than five seconds.

"Why don't you just go back to your own office, David?"

Seeing what he'd done, he started to put out a hand to her. He looked very proper in his banker's three-piece, the very image of a big-city detective. His hand continued to move toward her but then at the last moment he withdrew it.

"He's a ladies' man, Anna, and you've led a sheltered life, and he may well deceive you and you won't even know it."

"I'm a widow, David, not some little girl."

"But you've never met a man like him."

She thought a moment and then looked up at him. He looked so young and vulnerable, like a high school suitor holding roses, useless now that he'd been spurned. She reached up and kissed him on the cheek. "I don't know why I'm getting so mad, David. This is the first time you've ever shown any real emotion around me. I guess I should be flattered." Then she went back to her filing, knowing he was still watching her. "He's only going to be here one night, David, and then he'll be gone."

David said, blurted really, "Then it's time we had a talk."

"About what?"

"About . . . us."

"Oh, David. . . ."

"What?"

"It just wouldn't be right—us, I mean. We're just too different." She put out her hand and touched his shoulder. "I'm sorry, David, but I really haven't changed my mind. I like you a lot and consider you a very good friend, but—"

He drew himself up with what was left of his pride and said, "You're a very confused young woman, Anna. Very confused."

He was glaring at her as he backed out of the tiny office.

On the threshold, still glaring, he said once again, as if she might not have heard him the other two times, "Very confused."

EIGHT

"A pavilion dance will be held at the Cedar Springs hotel Wednesday May 10. A seven-piece orchestra will play."

He lay on his bed with a plate of fudge reading through the *Cedar Rapids Evening Gazette*, trying not to think about the impending arrival of the man who'd written the letter to his mother. The room was spacious with a white canopy bed and antiques from the Revolutionary War period which Mother had picked up on one of her many trips back East. The east window was open and you could feel the day's heat dying now at suppertime. It filled him inexplicably with a deep melancholy. Something wild and sad always filled him at day's end. . . .

His eyes drifted back to the notice about the pavilion dance. A few years ago he'd gone to one. He had worn his best cheviot suit and spent the night holding in his stomach until he got gas. Two or three times he'd nearly gotten up the nerve to cross the floor and ask one of the awkward young women—who never *got* asked—to dance. But he hadn't. His legs, at the last, would not carry him—and even if they had, his tongue would not have untangled enough to get the words out. So he sat in a corner and drank ginger fizzes without alcohol and just watched how the women swirled in the strong arms of their partners beneath the blue, yellow, and green Japanese lanterns, and how the breeze came off the clear blue Cedar ruffling the silver bottoms of the oak leaves, and how sweet and lonely the music was in the vast midwestern night. . . .

When he'd come home she'd known immediately that he'd done something he shouldn't have. She shrieked something about "women's perfume!" and slapped him and then it was into the cellar for two days, the first without any food or water at all. But even in the shadows below, he thought of the dance and one blond woman in particular who threw her head back so that you could see her perfect white neck, so erotic—

Putting down his fudge now, he picked up a pencil and circled the notation about the dance, which was still three days off. Perhaps if everything got straightened out with the man who wrote the letter he—

Then his hand touched the silver revolver lying next to him on the bed. Father's revolver.

He thought of the man in Elgin and the man in Ohio and the man in Indiana and the man in . . .

Through the open window he heard footsteps on the wide porch below and he knew instantly who was here.

Moving off the bed as quietly as possible, he went in his stocking feet to the bedroom door, eased it open and listened as his mother crossed the wide vestibule on the first floor and went to the front door.

She'd told him at all costs to stay up here—

He listened.

Susan Irene Eyles went to the door, opened it and stood there with a most imposing look on her face, one that had frightened governors, senators, continental dandies, bank presidents, theater stars, and any woman foolish enough to show interest in her son.

She said, "Yes?"

He was about what she'd expected, an ill-kempt man of dark hair and five o'clock shadow. He wore ministerial garb and looked ludicrous in it.

"You are Mrs. Eyles?"

"I am."

"I am the—"

"I know who you are."

He glanced around. On the distant sidewalk three children played hopscotch in the dusk and on the street an ancient, weary horse plodded by pulling an ice wagon.

"Aren't you going to invite me in?"

"Why would I?" Susan Irene Eyles said.

"Well, because—"

"Would you like to use my phone?"

"I beg your pardon?" The shabby man looked surprised. "Your phone?"

"Yes. To call the constable."

"The constable? But—"

"So, you are afraid to go to them," she said. "Just as I thought."

He glanced around once more as if they were being overheard. He still seemed quite perplexed by it all. "Maybe you misunderstood me, Mrs. Eyles. I don't *want* to go to the constable. I want five thousand dollars and then I'll just fade out of this town and—"

"You won't be getting a penny."

She almost smiled to herself. The cheap man looked so crushed when she spoke those words that the satisfaction was almost electric within her breast. She would savor this moment a long time. He had come here on his filthy business and she had defeated him, dared him to do the very thing he had threatened to do.

"But your son—"

"My son is a gentle, peaceful man who would never do any of the things you accuse him of. None of them."

"But he did. One of them I saw him do."

This time she did allow herself a smile. She stood in the doorway to her grand house, the frosted glass of the doors silver in the fading light, the Persian rug on which she stood still smelling sweetly of the cleaning she'd given it this afternoon, not trusting it to her maid. She stood there bold and confident and smiling.

"Then you would like to use my phone?"

"I really will go to the constable, ma'am," he said, "if for no other reason than it's my civic duty."

"Your civic duty." Her contempt by now was complete. She could scarcely stand to keep her eyes on him.

But he surprised her by putting a single foot on the threshold and moving so suddenly forward that she had no choice but to back up. She certainly did not want to come into any sort of physical contact with the man.

Then he set a second foot inside and before she quite knew what had happened, he had closed the door softly behind him.

He now stood, bold as she'd been, in the center of the vestibule, staring up as everyone always did at the vast chandelier that she had brought back with her from Paris in the summer of '61 when she'd still thought that Clinton might yet get rid of his mistress and that things would be all right between them.

By now the would-be minister was appraising the rest of the house, the staircase sweeping to the two floors above, the flocked wallpaper, the open sliding doors revealing the vast parlor with its fireplace and wall-length bookcases and period furniture.

Then Reverend Parsons's eyes dropped back to her. He grinned. "You sure had me going there for a minute."

"What?"

"You. The way you act." He whistled. "You're a real scary woman when you want to be." He shook his head. "I mean, I nearly turned tail and ran, to be perfectly honest and all."

"I want you to leave or I'll call the police."

"Oh, now, you ain't going to do that."

"I most certainly will."

"That's just part of your game."

"It's no game."

"Sure it is. It's the game rich people always play with poor people. They take this high-and-mighty attitude and then just watch the poor people scatter." He winked at her. In his Roman collar the wink was obscene. "And most of the time it works because inside there isn't a minute goes by that we don't get scared of somethin'—a cop comin' by, or some street tough comin' down on us, or not havin' enough money for our next meal." He shrugged, seeming to be vastly relaxed now. "And that's how I was back there on the porch. Watchin' you, I mean. I thought, boy, I sure have come to the wrong woman because I'm not goin' to get any satisfaction at all. No, sir, no satisfaction at all. But then you know what? I looked over your shoulder and I saw him standin' there and I knew, oh I just knew, that things were just about like I sized 'em up. Inside, Mrs. Eyles, you're just as scared as I am."

And with that, despite herself, not wanting to concede the man any power over her at all, she turned to find her son hiding in the shadows of the closet, watching them. Fat, dressed in nothing more than a bosom shirt and dark trousers with red suspenders and red socks, he simply stared at the Reverend Parsons, keeping his hands mysteriously behind his back as he did so.

She turned back to Parsons. "I want you to leave."

"I want five thousand dollars."

"As I said, you won't get a cent."

"You ever see a hangin', Mrs. Eyles?"

"You won't—"

"They'll have to build a special gallows. He's a mighty big boy. They'll want to make sure his neck snaps right away— otherwise, he could dangle there a long time and just slowly strangle and—"

And that's when James Eyles bolted from the closet. In what seemed like blinding speed for someone his size, he crossed the vestibule and produced from behind his back the silver revolver that had belonged to his father and, before either his mother or Parsons could stop him, he'd brought the handle of the pistol down on Parsons's forehead, opening up a small gash.

What happened next, Susan Irene Eyles could not have imagined even in a nightmare.

The boy she'd so carefully raised to be her most gentle and civilized companion had become an animal she did not recognize. He grabbed Parsons by the jacket of his minister's suit and slammed him back against the door, at which point James began clubbing him with huge and unyielding fists, and Parsons started to bleed and whimper.

James smashed the man in the face and then in the stomach and brought a knee up to the man's groin. When Parsons slipped to his knees, James once again brought the handle of the pistol down across the top of his head.

By now, of course, Susan Irene Eyles had begun screaming. She threw herself at her son, trying to pull hims off Parsons. James turned to her just once and she looked into the eyes of a stranger, a terrifying one.

With a single hand, he grabbed her by the waist and flung her back toward the closet.

Then he resumed beating Parsons.

As she slammed into the polished banister, crying out as the jutting wood cracked her back, she saw the broom that the maid had left standing in the corner before she had left for her night off.

All Susan Irene Eyles could think of was stopping her son before he killed Parsons.

Moving as quickly as she could, she went over and grabbed the broom and then got directly behind his back.

By now James was kicking Parsons in the ribs.

She brought the broom handle down clean across his cranium. He started to turn back to her and she struck him again. Finally, cursing, he collapsed.

She stood in that awful moment—the sound of James's huge body hitting the floor, Parsons sobbing, and her own breath coming in gasps—seeing that her entire life was on the verge of collapse.

James would be made to face the constable and there might indeed be a hanging and she would not have a companion and—

She rushed to the downstairs bathroom and soaked big towels for Parsons and then rushed back and began daubing the blood away.

"You bitch," he said as she began trying to make him feel better.

"I just want to help," she said.

"The price just went up to ten thousand," he said. He was crying.

"Don't you worry. You'll get ten thousand dollars. I promise you."

With that, Parsons, who had looked miserable just a moment before, seemed much improved. True, his eye was blackened and two of his teeth had been knocked loose and he still clutched his groin.

But he wore the unmistakable smile of a man who had triumphed.

Oh, yes, the good fake Reverend Parsons had triumphed indeed.

"I wonder if you'd do me a favor?" she said when she'd finished tending to Parsons.

His voice was hostile. "Why should I do you a favor?"

"You want your money, don't you?"

"What's the favor?"

"Help me move him."

"To where."

She sighed. It was an outsize and dramatic sigh, one she'd practiced for decades. "To the cellar, where else? To the cellar."

NINE

"Hello, Boyd."

"Hello, Stephen. I sure do appreciate you coming."

"Came as soon as I heard." He paused. Put out his hand and touched it to his friend's shoulder. In the war the Union troops had seemed particularly susceptible to malaria the deeper they pushed into the South, and Fuller had seen many men die of the disease. You got white and sweaty and lost weight and looked dead well before your time.

Boyd Haskell lay in a ward on the north end of St. Luke's hospital, the first stars of evening in the window, and looked very much as if he had malaria. But what he really had was a heart disease that Fuller did not understand in the least. All he knew was that the doctors predicted Boyd would be dead by the end of the week. The room smelled of rubbing alcohol and cleaning solvent on the floor. There were eight beds. Everything was immaculate and big and impressive. It was a very good hospital, even by big city standards. Nurses in crisp white uniforms came in and out with great professional decorum, bending over the beds surrounding Boyd Haskell, seeing how the other men were doing. Fuller had been told that any visit more than five minutes would exhaust Haskell, so Fuller was prepared to speak quickly.

He said, "I took your baseball that time."

"What?" Haskell, his thinning dark hair plastered to his head with sweat, raised worn brown eyes to Fuller.

"I took your baseball. Back in the orphanage when we were ten."

"You serious?"

"Yep."

"You never stole nothin' in your life, Stephen."

"You're right. Except for that time. I saw that new baseball you won downtown at the Fourth of July celebration and it was like I couldn't help myself." He reached into the pocket of his coat and brought out a fancy stitched, brand-new baseball and set it on the night table next to the bed.

"Hell, Stephen. You're being silly."

"Just settling a debt."

Boyd Haskell reached over and picked up the baseball and hefted it in his hand. Easy enough at that moment for Fuller to imagine Boyd a kid again on a cool April morning, the first bats of spring cracking the first baseballs. They'd been like brothers.

"Guess I don't have to tell you how much I care about you," Fuller said.

Boyd looked up and smiled. "Guess you don't. And you know I feel the same way."

"Was sorry to hear about your wife and boy."

Boyd's eyes narrowed as the past assaulted him. "Goddamn kerosene stoves. You know how they can be."

"I'm sorry anyway."

The tears in Boyd's eyes were obvious. Fuller had to look away.

Boyd Haskell said, "Never had a friend I read about in the papers before."

"The papers like fancy stories."

"A gunfighter." He seemed to speak with a combination of awe and just a small bit of disapproval.

"That's what I mean by fancy stories. I never was a gunfighter."

"You weren't?"

"No. Just a lawman who moved from town to town and every once in a while I'd run up against one of the old legends who'd managed to stay alive somehow and then he'd get drunk or I'd get drunk and it'd lead to one of us drawing down and I was always just lucky enough to stay alive."

"Hell's bells. But the papers—"

"You know how they are. They love fancy stories, just like I said."

Boyd stared at his friend and then a wily grin broke his face. "You sure you didn't give those newspapermen a little encouragement?"

"Well . . ."

"I mean, you always liked a fancy story yourself, Stephen."

Fuller laughed at himself. "Well, I probably did drop a few broad hints from time to time about just how good with a gun I really was."

"And dropped a few broad hints about knowing Wyatt Earp and the Reno Brothers and people like that."

"I suppose I might have done something like that after I had a few tastes of rye."

"How's that going?"

Suddenly the festive air of the conversation was gone. They were in a white room with sick men and the spring stars seemed more distant and cold than ever.

Fuller said, "Fine."

"Mrs. Emory called me a few years back, over to the hardware store. She said you wrote her a letter from one of those hospitals where they put drunkards."

Fuller sighed. "Yeah, I guess I did."

"Kind of funny you writing Mrs. Emory."

Fuller nodded. "You know, all the time we were at the orphanage, I never did care for her much. Too stern. Too many rules. Things like that. But for some reason when I was in that hospital—"

"I know what you mean. Till she died last summer, I always went over and visited her every Sunday afternoon. Guess it was like goin' to visit my mother or something."

Fuller stared down at Boyd and said, "You've got a nice life here in Cedar Rapids. Your job at the Star Wagon Works, Mrs. Emory—"

For the first time, Boyd showed a flash of bitterness. You always saw it in people who were dying and knew they were dying. The bitterness, born of fear, was just part of the process. "All in the past, Stephen. All in the past."

And then the bitterness was gone and he laughed. "You know what I was thinkin' about the other day?"

"What?"

"How you always said we were like dogs in a pound when the people came to look us over for adoption."

Fuller laughed throatily. "They must've been damned sensible people—they wouldn't take either one of us."

Boyd hefted the baseball again. "Who'd want a kid who stole baseballs?"

"And who'd want a kid who couldn't ride a horse?" Fuller said, referring to the fact that no matter how hard he tried, Boyd Haskell just couldn't seem to get along with horses. He always got thrown.

Boyd said, softly, "So you on the wagon?"

"More or less."

"Don't think you can do it that way, my friend."

Fuller grinned but it was an empty grin. "Well, let's say I'm more on the wagon than less. How's that?"

Boyd reached up and took his hand. "I remember my old man. How the hooch got to him. It's a miserable way to die." He tapped his heart. "Even a worse way to die than this. You got some life left in you, Stephen. You stay dry, all right?" He smiled. "You remember Mrs. Emory always figured I was older than you by about two years or so, so I get to give you orders. And that's one order I'm givin' you for sure."

A nurse came in and touched Fuller's arm. "Time, Mr. Fuller," she whispered.

When she left, Boyd said, "You came a long way."

"I wanted to."

"You been the best friend I ever had. All the time after my wife and boy got killed, I just kept thinkin' of you, Stephen, and it gave me strength. How we got through the orphanage and everything."

Fuller was going to cry and he knew it but he didn't want to cry here. It would be selfish and only make things worse for Boyd.

"You're going to be around for a lot longer than you think," Fuller said, wanting to leave on a good strong note.

But Boyd said, "End of the week, the way the docs figure. Hell, I already made my last confession." He tapped his heart again. "Something like this, you just don't have any warning." He looked white and old and sad and Fuller wondered how long he could hold back the tears.

They shook hands. They both seemed reluctant to let go.

Boyd must have seen the tears coming in Fuller's eyes because he withdrew his hand and quickly changed the subject. He snatched the baseball and said, "The least you could've done was get it autographed by one of the White Sox for me."

"You like the White Sox?"

"Sure. Don't you?"

"Not especially."

Boyd looked over at the old man in the next bed. "This guy doesn't like the White Sox?"

The old man, picking up the joke, said, "Seems like he's the one who's sick. Not us."

The rest of the ward laughed.

Boyd nodded to the doorway. "The nurse is back. Hovering."

"I know."

"You do what I say, Stephen. About John Barleycorn."

"I hear you, Stephen."

"And thanks for the baseball."

"You bet."

Now he knew he was losing control completely. This man and Mrs. Emory were the closest he'd ever come to having a family. His heart hammered and sweat collected in his armpits and on the bottoms of his feet. He was afraid he wouldn't be able to talk at all. "Take care of yourself, Boyd."

"You do the same."

"Maybe when I'm in Chicago I'll take in a White Sox game. Maybe it'll change my mind."

Boyd grinned. "That's the first sensible thing you've said all day."

The nurse was there again, gently, at his sleeve.

"So long, Boyd."

"So long, Stephen."

They stared at each other for what Fuller knew would be the last time and then he let the nurse lead him as if he were a child down past the other beds and out into the corridor.

He felt as if his body temperature had dropped several degrees within the past few minutes. His teeth were chattering.

The nurse helped him over to a chair where he sat and stared out at the stars. He thought of Boyd in there dying and then he knew, knew with terrible and humiliating certainty, where he legs would lead him once he left St. Luke's.

Knew just where they'd lead him.

TEN

There was a wall safe in the den where she kept both currency and certain jewelry of which she was unduly fond.

She made him wait out in the vestibule and then she went in to get the ten thousand dollars in cash that was his demand.

She still could not get from her mind the sight of her son James seizing the man named Parsons and nearly killing him with his fists.

She could not recognize her son in the beast she'd seen before her and her glimpse of him that way cleared up any doubts about his ability to kill people. Now she wondered just how many people he really had killed on his travels.

As she opened the safe, she thought of the options—very few indeed—open to her now. She would have to move quickly and deftly to protect her son. Taking up permanent residence in Europe was the only answer, of course. Parsons would take the money and drink and whore through it and then when it was gone, he would be back for more.

But Susan Irene Eyles was going to surprise him.

Because by the time Parsons came back for more, she and James would be long gone.

Long gone.

She opened the safe, withdrew a large stack of currency, counted through it until she had the proper amount, and closed the safe.

Gathering herself, throwing her shoulders back so that her matronly body was even more forbidding, she marched out of the den and down to the corridor where Parsons waited. The way he paced, it was obvious how nervous he was, even when he had the upper hand. It told you all you needed to know about his character. She even felt a tiny note of satisfaction on seeing how bruised his face was. But then she thought of what an animal her son had been and—

Without realizing what she was doing, she slapped Parsons once very hard directly across the mouth.

The blow was sufficient to knock him back into the door.

He started to speak but she held up her hand.

"Here is your money. I never want to see or hear of you again. If I do, I will have you killed. Do you understand?"

But she didn't wait for an answer, or a nod of recognition. She simply handed him the currency, turned him abruptly around by his shoulders, opened the door and pushed him out into the night.

The door slamming behind him sounded like a rifle shot.

ELEVEN

"You want a schooner?" the barman asked.

Fuller glanced around the tavern. It was packed with men of the merchant class, in good suits and bowlers and silk brocaded vests. The place was even fancier than Fuller had expected, with a hardwood floor, Rochester lamps, and a mahogany bar that had obviously been polished to reflect the owner's pride. The place smelled of sweat, cigars, and the yeast in the beer.

Fuller glanced down at his trembling hand. "Maybe just a glass of water, if you wouldn't mind."

The barman, a squat man with hair parted down the center and slicked to either side, wiped his hands on a pure white apron and said, "You're Fuller, ain't you? Stephen Fuller."

Fuller sighed. "I guess I am, after all, aren't I?"

"Don't want no trouble in here."

"Won't be any."

The barman said, "You're older than I thought you'd be."

Fuller laughed. "I'm older than *I* thought I'd be."

His joke seemed to relax both of them.

The barman offered him a cigar, which Fuller declined. "Get some ruffians in here sometimes. That's all I meant by trouble. Seems like people'd be bound to pick a fight with you."

Fuller nodded. He was looking beyond the barman now. He was seeing Boyd Haskell in the hospital bed. So pale. So sweaty. A frail dying animal.

Clearing his throat, Fuller said, "Why don't you make that a schooner and a shot?"

The barman laughed. "Now that's more like it. And I'll tell you what. First round's on house."

Just one, Fuller thought.

These days, now, he could control it.

It wouldn't be as in the past when he—

The barman set the schooner and the shot of whiskey on the counter in front of Fuller. In the light of the Rochester lamps, the whiskey seemed to glow from within—a taunting, beckoning light pulling Stephen Fuller to it.

He picked up the shot glass and threw it straight back.

Tears of rage and self-loathing and a head-spinning satisfaction filled Fuller.

The barman, laughing again, filled up the shot glass and said, "So you knew Wyatt Earp, huh?"

Lifting the schooner, Fuller said, "There was a long time when he was one of my best friends." He paused, the way they always wanted him to pause because people like the barman here always wanted stories to be dramatic. He had a flash of Boyd Haskell lying back there in the hospital, just waiting for that one last pain to arc across his chest—

"Met Wyatt in Abilene, actually," Fuller said, and then, as sometimes happened, he sort of stood back from himself, almost like a stranger observing himself, to hear just exactly what was going to come out of his mouth. Because sometimes the tales got so fascinating, and took such unexpected turns, that Fuller got just as interested in his own words as his audience (be it a sole barman or a whole saloon).

"Abilene, huh?" the barman said, kid-excited and kid-delighted. "Hear that was a mighty tough place."

"Tough doesn't begin to cover it. Doesn't begin at all," Stephen Fuller said.

He threw back his second shot and began to tell his tale. Soon there were at least half a dozen other men who'd gathered around, kid-excited, too.

"He didn't say?"

"I'm sorry, Anna. He didn't say."

"But where—?" Then Anna Tolan snapped her fingers and

said, "I'd better get down to the phone." Mrs. Goldman had had her telephone—a small brown box with a big silver bell and a small black receiver hanging from its side—installed just last month. It held a position of both reverence and novelty down in the hall just off the vestibule.

Anna, gathering the skirts of her pinafore, ran down the steps and picked up the receiver, and then ran her finger down the list of phone numbers Mrs. Goldman had clipped from the *Evening Gazette.*

She found the number for St. Luke's hospital.

Mrs. Goldman stood by anxiously—"I didn't know he had troubles with alcohol," Mrs. Goldman had said earlier in explaining why she hadn't managed to keep him here till Anna had returned—listening as Anna talked, first to a nurse and then a doctor about Stephen Fuller's appearance at St. Luke's.

Finally, hanging up, she said, "They don't know where he went after he visited Boyd Haskell, of course."

"I feel this is all my fault."

"Oh, Mrs. Goldman," Anna said, taking the older woman's hands gently. "Of course it isn't. It's my fault."

"Your fault?"

"I should have known better than to leave him. And if David Peary ever finds out—" She shook her head. She knew she was letting her pride overcome her. If Fuller went off and got drunk and got in trouble when he was supposedly in Anna's charge, then Peary—not to mention the chief—would subtly suggest that Anna (or any woman for that matter) was not capable of being a bona fide constable. "I've got to go find him, Mrs. Goldman."

"But where?"

Anna sighed. "I'm afraid I know where."

"A tavern?"

"Exactly."

"I should have locked his door."

"It wouldn't have done any good."

"It wouldn't?"

"There's one thing about drunkards, Mrs. Goldman. No

matter what kind of obstacle you put in their way, they manage to find their alcohol."

"The poor devils."

"Yes, Mrs. Goldman," Anna said. "That's exactly what they are. Poor devils."

And with that she left the boardinghouse, running down the steps to her Imperial, and then pedaling off toward downtown.

She would have to search for Stephen Fuller tavern by tavern. There was no other way.

By seven o'clock that evening, Parsons had dropped in on a steam bath, a restaurant, and three taverns. (Also a haberdasher, the S. B. Dix Company, having decided that for a night on the town the religious getup was just too conspicuous.) The effects of the beating James Eyles had inflicted on him were beginning to recede somewhat. True, the crimp in his right shoulder had not left and his left leg was not feeling much better, but his fingers worked fine now and the headache (thanks to the steam bath) had gone entirely.

A long night stretched ahead of him. A cabbie down by the railroad depot (where Parsons had purchased a ticket for the morning train to Chicago) had told him where young girls could be had, and so the starry spring evening held great and abiding promise for him.

He was thinking of this as he patted the money inside his new suit jacket (he was becoming fixated with that most reassuring of lumps, touching it every few seconds, as if some terrible magic would take it from him) as he crossed the threshold into a very impressive-looking tavern.

He immediately liked the gentlemanly atmosphere of the place—the fancy flocked wallpaper and the shiny spittoons—and the soft glow of the Rochester lamps.

Ordinarily, he felt intimidated by such places. He was neither educated nor successful and quite often places such as these were inhabited by men all too eager to let you know that they were both.

But tonight, with that very special lump in his new suit coat, and several whiskeys already warming his stomach on top of a good steak dinner, he felt a wonderful confidence in himself, as if he'd be quite capable of sitting down across the table from President Grover Cleveland himself and carrying on a conversation.

He had just stepped up to the bar and started to order a drink when he noticed that, at the other end of the long mahogany bar, a small group had gathered. The group was listening to a man. The group seemed quite intent, almost reverent.

Curious, Parsons moved down the bar to hear more.

One time, two years ago, he had tried breaking out of the cellar by running up the steps and hurtling himself against the door.

The result had been a terrible, spreading bruise on his shoulder that had kept him in pain for nearly two weeks.

What he had not realized till that night was that Mother had had the door double-reinforced with two-by-fours and then covered with steel. In addition to this it was locked with a dead bolt which virtually no amount of pressure could move.

He was down in the cellar now. It smelled of coal and mildew and her fruit preserves.

Earlier, in anger, he'd caught a mouse and squeezed it in his hand until he felt its ribs grind into nothingness and its warm vomit-like innards begin to run out of its tiny mouth.

Then he'd tossed the little rodent away and begun sulking again over his plan.

Tonight, somehow, he was going to find and kill the man called Parsons.

This afternoon, when he'd flung himself on the man, the flash that always overcame him during violent moments blinded him again. Then as Mother shrieked hysterically, he'd realized that of all the people he'd killed, he hadn't really hated any of them.

They'd called him names, or joked about his size, or whispered about him, but he hadn't really hated them. It had just been momentary anger.

But Parsons—

No, Parsons was somebody he truly wanted to kill.

But Parsons—

He was thinking about this when he heard the dead bolt of the slanted cellar door being slid free.

Mother.

He huddled back in the corner of the cellar. Perhaps he should not have crushed that mouse, he thought. In some ways he was very much like that tiny animal himself. A creature of night and shadow, despised by supposedly decent and civilized human beings.

He wondered if Mother had any inkling.

When he'd been a small boy, he sometimes wondered if she couldn't actually read his mind, the way swamis at circuses claimed they could read minds. He would see a girl and think dirty thoughts and Mother would glance at him and he would know she knew. Or he would try to sneak off to the park to play with the other boys—"vulgarians" Mother always called them—and this power look would come into her eyes and he would go back up to his room and lie on his bed and read the religious books Mother kept there for him.

But he wondered if she knew now what lay ahead. He could scarcely believe it himself. But he knew in his most secret heart that this was an inevitable act. Indeed, the most inevitable act of his life.

The door squeaked open.

He saw a field of stars against a blue-black night and felt a cool breath of spring evening. There would be silver dew on the green grass and the tips of the trees would look burnished with moonlight. There would be the bark of distant dogs and the sweet smell of apple blossoms. There would be girls—

(He wondered whatever had happened to ninth grade Karen Standers. He dreamed of her still. Still . . .)

She carried a lantern and the light it cast gave the cellar the look of a deep and dank cave. She held the lantern at face level and said, "You come out here, now, James. We need to pack tonight. We're leaving for Europe in the morning. Very early."

And then he was there, all right, a giant chunk of anthracite coal in his right hand.

She turned, startled, because he'd come up from behind her—but before she could turn around completely, he had almost smashed in the side of her head with the anthracite.

He continued smashing her until she looked very much the way the mouse had.

Very much.

TWELVE

The Imperial was a "beaut" ("beaut" being a favorite word of young boys in that green, blooming spring) with, among its many enviable features, genuine single tube tires from the Akron India Tire Company, rubber pedals, and a tool bag with tire pump, repair outfit, oiler, and wrench. The Imperial had received four coats of enamel, was striped for beauty, and varnished to prevent scratching. In all, it weighed twenty-three pounds, and when Anna took it up in the hills north of the town, looking over the sweeping curve of the Cedar, she felt a real kinship with birds, especially when she went down steep hills with her arms and legs stuck straight out, the Imperial seeming to guide her by its own volition.

Ordinarily, she felt the same pride in the Imperial when she rode it around town. Now, however, she was too concerned with finding Stephen Fuller to be aware of who might be looking for her.

She started her search over by the Ely Building. Because he had not eaten supper at Mrs. Goldman's, Anna felt he might stop in one of the many restaurants that lined the downtown and were known as far away as Chicago for their cuisine.

In two different places she thought she'd glimpsed him. Her heart hammering, she'd started over to the diner she'd mistaken for him—and then realized that he was not her man.

In one place, an Italian restaurant, the owner mused with a finger and thumb clamped to his jaw, saying he wondered if such a man might not have been in here an hour ago but then he described the man in more detail—he was the kind of witness constables loved; he remembered everything—and in doing so he made mention of a mole on the man's right cheek.

Which made him obviously not Fuller.

She tried the taverns next, starting down by the tracks that effectively cut the city in half.

In most places she got the same initial reaction. Men emboldened by a few—or many—schooners would turn to look at the very pretty woman standing in the doorway. Then, as she'd come in, they'd see the big silver badge riding the breast of her pinafore—and then they wouldn't know quite how to act, social sense struggling with biology.

The workingmen's places were filled with the clack of pool balls and gruff but friendly arguments over pinochle games. The merchants' places featured billiard tables and player pianos, except for those associated with restaurants, in which the bar was as fancy as the dining area.

There were the usual sights—some men drinking well and having a good time, others drinking poorly and being argumentative or giving evidence that deep within them was abiding pain. The latter were those Anna usually saw at one time or another in the jail in the cruel bright morning when hangover and guilt collided within one head.

Over on Second Street, just after entering a place called "Golden Hours," she felt a hand on her shoulder.

She felt an inexplicable girlish hope that the hand would belong to Fuller and that there, sober, he would stand.

But when she turned around, she saw a very different man. Detective David Peary. He frowned. "Do you really think it's proper to come into a place like this, Anna?" He indicated the men along the bar who were staring at her.

She wanted to say something sarcastic—something that would turn the moment to her advantage—but she seemed struck dumb. "I—" she began to say.

Then, more confident than ever, Peary hooked his left thumb in his vest, hoisted his schooner for a drink in his other hand, and then said, giving a little satisfied "ah" over the beer, "You haven't lost Fuller have you?"

"Lost Fuller? I don't know what you're talking about."

Peary, obviously sensing that something was disturbing Anna, said, "You know I was against this whole thing from the beginning."

"I know."

"A man like that should not be allowed in Cedar Rapids. Let alone left to roam around free."

"He isn't roaming around free," Anna said.

"Then where is he?"

"He's—" She gulped. She was terrible at lying. Terrible. "He's at Mrs. Goldman's asleep."

Peary's eyes narrowed. "Are you all right, Anna?"

"Yes. I'm fine." But she'd said it far too quickly.

"Then what are you doing in a place like this?"

"I might ask the same of you."

"I, in case you haven't noticed, am a man. And you haven't answered my question."

"I came in here to get a spafizz." A spafizz was a strawberry drink favored by Cedar Rapidians.

"They don't sell spafizzes in a place like this."

"Then I came to the wrong place."

"You know they don't sell spafizzes in here." He assessed her over the rim of his mug again. "You're not telling me the truth, are you?"

She hesitated a moment too long.

"Where is he, Anna?"

She sighed, cast eyes to the floor. She had not felt any lonelier or more isolated since the night of her husband's wake.

"I'm not sure," she mumbled.

"What?"

She raised her head. "I said I'm not sure."

"Oh, wonderful. Then he *is* roaming around free."

"Did it ever occur to you that maybe he's not what you think he is?"

"He's killed a dozen men hasn't he?"

"He was a lawman, don't forget."

"On the frontier, Anna, being a lawman was little more than a license to steal and kill."

"He went to see his friend at the hospital. His dying friend."

"And then he went where?"

"That's—" Her voice faltered.

"You were going to watch him, Anna. That was the bargain you made with the chief."

"I realize that."

He sounded like a scolding teacher. "You were supposed to watch him and now look what's happened."

"Nothing's happened, David. I'll find him and bring him back to Mrs. Goldman's and then in the morning I'll put him on the train and then he'll leave Cedar Rapids and everybody will forget all about him and that will be that."

But Peary shook his head. "Meanwhile, the city has to put up with a drunken gunfighter on the prowl."

"You don't know he's drunk."

"I don't? You heard what the chief said about his drinking problems." Then he smiled bitterly at her. "And if you weren't afraid he was drinking, you'd never be checking out taverns."

"I'm not—"

"Of course you are. Now it all makes sense. Why would you come into a place like this? Because you're looking for Fuller and you're afraid he's in a tavern somewhere getting pickled and that he'll shoot somebody."

The last thing she wanted to happen happened just then. Her eyes filled with tears of anger. But it didn't matter what prompted the tears. He'd just see them as a sign of womanly weakness.

Seeing them, he moved back a few feet. Men never knew what to do when women cried. He shook his head. Something like pity came into his eyes. "Anna, look, I—" He shook his head. "Dammit, Anna, why don't you listen to me—"

"Oh, David—"

"We could have a fine life. You could give up the department and we could get married and have a nice house out on Third Avenue just down from my brother's and—"

She wanted to resent him for all this.

She wanted to tell herself that he was being the worst sort of man, the sort who had no trust at all in a woman's abilities to take on real responsibilities and—

She startled them both by leaning into him and kissing him on the cheek.

"You know something, David?"

Being kissed in public this way had caused him to blush. "What?" he said. But his voice was croaky, barely there.

"You're a nice man even when you don't want to be." She touched his sleeve. "I know you think you're saying what I need to hear—that I should get married and settle down. And you know what?'

"What?"

"A part of me wants to. A part of me is very lonely and very frightened. But that's just a part of me. The other part wants to be a constable."

"Then keep on working as a matron and—"

"Not a matron, David. A constable. With full rights and responsibilities. I want to be like Goron—"

Now his frown came full measure. "Goron. You'll never be—"

"Who says I won't? It's not impossible. I'm studying his methods and—"

David shook his head. "He's a French police chief who got lucky a few times solving crimes and now a lot of very silly people have made a big thing over his 'method.' " Now, apparently no longer so embarrassed to be seen showing affection in front of onlookers down the long bar before the big painting of a nude woman carefully covered up with wisps of fog—he took Anna's hand and said, "Then be a constable,

Anna. But forget about all the rest—and take me up on my offer."

Now it was her turn to shake her head. "David, you know how the magazines always talk about people who aren't 'compatible.'"

"Magazines," he said bitterly.

"Well, we're not compatible. Sometimes I wish we were but—" And now all she could do was shrug. "I'm sorry, David. I really am."

She looked at the big Ingraham on the wall.

Given the patterns of men with drinking problems, she knew that Stephen Fuller would by now most likely be well on his way to drunkenness.

"I need to go now, David," she said gently.

She hadn't noticed till this moment but he rocked slightly on his feet. David Peary, unthinkable as it was, was a bit tipsy himself.

"You're going to go looking for Fuller, aren't you?"

"Yes."

"Then I'll tell you where to look," he said.

"Where?"

"The gutter."

He turned angrily away and went back down the bar.

The onlookers would be talking about this little argument the rest of the night.

THIRTEEN

He waited until dark and then he took her out of the cellar and buried her in the backyard.

Because there were many neighborhood dogs—in particular one very inquisitive Great Dane—he made the grave four feet deep (digging until his hands ran with blood) and then covered her with rocks.

He then stood under the panorama of stars, the fragrance of spring roses on the air, wondering what to feel.

He knew what he *should* feel.

He had, after all, just killed his mother.

He *should* feel intolerable remorse. The sort he felt many times when she'd put him down in the cellar for being a bad boy. Then, he had sobbed and loathed himself so much that he'd beaten his head against the supporting beams of the cellar until lumps were raised on his cranium.

But now . . .

He looked down at the pile of rocks beneath which was Mother and felt—nothing.

Not a thing.

And he wanted to. He wanted the release of tears, of outright weeping.

He thought of all the things she'd loved, and hoped that the images of these things would shatter him.

Of Winslow Homer's watercolor "Women Sewing."

Of Debussy.

Of her George III candlesticks.

Of how she'd tousle his hair as he ate the big plate of fudge she was forever making him.

But—

—nothing.

Perhaps, he sensed, there would be time for tears and remorse once his business was finished in Cedar Rapids and he was gone for good.

Then, during a period of reflection, he would realize the enormity of what he'd done and feel the shame and guilt he should.

But there was the one thing left to do tonight.

One man knew his secret.

One man.

Now, standing beneath the stars, the quarter moon almost unnaturally bright, he felt again the pleasure of this afternoon when he'd begun to thrash Parsons.

Parsons. . . .

James Eyles looked back to the house, the cupolas and

spires and gingerbread work that made it such a distinguished Victorian.

He would take the silver pistol that had belonged to his father and go searching for Parsons.

He glanced down once again to the pile of rocks beneath which Mother lay.

Mother.

Someday he would regret what he had done. He knew he would.

He just knew it.

FOURTEEN

Parsons said, "That man is a liar."

He said this at a time when the alcohol had made him more than a little dizzy and even still more belligerent. In third grade he had beaten up a boy with a savagery that forever after made other boys walk shy of him. Two things had not been taken into account about that particular fight: the boy was of much slighter frame than Parsons and Parsons had secretly folded a rock into his hand so that when he struck the other boy it was with much greater force than his fist alone could have delivered. But somehow Parsons himself had begun to believe the story that he was tough when, in fact, he was not. Take the time in Indianapolis—in those days he was disguised as a drummer—the Indian had challenged Parsons's slurs. The Indian had slapped him at least half a dozen times before Parsons, humiliated in front of the others in the tavern, had been able to cry out for mercy. Or the time in Cleveland—then all dressed up as a newspaperman—when the businessman had taken exception to the attention Parsons had paid to the man's wife. The businessman, not a virile looking sort at all, had punched Parsons so hard in the solar plexus that Parsons had not only doubled over but vomited right there on the floor. Not that any of this made a difference when alcohol affected him. On the right night, and after a number of drinks, Parsons was always filled with this cumbersome sense of sheer brute power—a power crying out to be used. As, inevitably, it was used when Parsons would argue too violently with this man's political opinion or that man's religious belief (from his parents he had inherited a somewhat inexplicable dislike of Lutherans).

Tonight the object of his scorn was the tall man who had gathered around him a small crowd of men who were every bit as doting as a group of young boys around a cousin just returned from some exotic place, the golden sands of Arabia or the vast muddy power of the Amazon.

"He's a liar," Parsons said again.

He had already begun to slur his words as the two drummers close to him at the bar obviously noted.

"Don't you know who he is?"

"Of course I know who he is. He's a liar."

"I'm serious," one of the two drummers said.

"So am I."

"He's Stephen Fuller."

"Excuse me for not being impressed." At this point Parsons once again patted the breast pocket of his suit. Ten thousand sweet dollars.

"He's killed twelve men," the first drummer said.

"I heard he's killed twenty," said the other drummer.

The first drummer glanced at Parsons and made a clucking sound. "There you go, friend. Twenty men."

"The hell," Parsons said.

"The hell yourself," the second drummer said. He was as drunk as Parsons and getting just as irritable.

At this point the group gathered around Stephen Fuller laughed heartily. There were also a few "oooh" sounds. Fuller was rolling, the stories getting wilder and ever more intriguing. From here you could hear Fuller mention the name of Jesse James. The James brothers stories were especially good, Fuller having the ability—and think of what he could have done if he'd actually ever met the James boys—of making the Missouri saga both humorous, daring, and heart-breaking.

The James brothers stories, which, of course, shifted slightly each time he told them—got better actually—were the best tales in his entire repertoire.

"He couldn't have known Jesse James in Missouri that spring," Parsons said.

"And why not?" asked one of the drummers. The two men, both plump, both in checkered suits, exchanged derisive glances.

"Because Jesse James wasn't in Missouri spring of sixty-nine."

"And just where was he?"

"Alabama."

The two drummers hooted. "Jesse James? Alabama?"

"You damn right. He was down there robbing banks."

"Bullroar."

A smug smile filled Parsons's face. "I'm right and I'm going to tell that loudmouth at the end of the bar that I'm right."

"I surely wouldn't do that, mister," the first drummer said.

"I surely wouldn't," the second drummer agreed.

With great dignity—dignity coming easier to a man with ten thousand dollars (minus a few hundred for duds and eats and the steam bath and all the rest)—Parsons picked up his schooner and shot and proceeded to the end of the bar.

He had to edge his way through the group that was all back-slaps and chortles and kid-shouts of glee.

Finally he worked his way right up to the man himself—the supposedly notorious Stephen Fuller of whom Parsons had only vaguely heard—and then when he got there he lifted his shot glass up and splashed its contents right across Fuller's face.

Fuller, stunned, began to wipe off his face as Parsons, emboldened by his own act, said, "Sir, I accuse you of being a liar."

In his mind, Parsons imagined himself to be a fine southern

gentleman gallantly slap-of-glove-style challenging a base opponent to a duel. Magnificent. . . .

All he was aware of suddenly was that people were moving away from him and that he was standing there alone, face to face with Stephen Fuller.

He was drunker suddenly than he'd realized, his stomach bloated, his senses spinning, his stance uncertain now, and then he recalled the Indian in Indianapolis and the businessman in Cleveland and what they had done to him.

He glanced down suddenly to see the man named Stephen Fuller do something terrible and beyond comprehension—

—Parsons wanting to scream that he was sorry for what he'd done and said—

Stephen Fuller easing back the side of his suit coat and reaching for his gun.

FIFTEEN

"Please, look carefully."

"By God, that is him."

"He's here then?"

"Been here. Don't think he's here now."

"When would that have been?"

The bartender of the beer garden shrugged. He was plump and Austrian, with puffy red cheeks and intense blue eyes and a huge cleft in his chin. He was bald and a black cigar kept vigil in the left corner of his mouth. Anna imagined the man could probably eat his supper without taking the cigar out of his mouth.

The bartender thought and said, "An hour, hour and a half ago." He waved his hand to the beer garden that sat on the bank of the Cedar. A polka band played festively and paper Japanese lanterns wavered in the wind, vivid green and yellow and pink against the velvet night sky. Women with golden hair done up in braids, with sprigs of fresh violets woven right into their hair, danced with husbands and suitors and boys who would do till somebody better came along. The waiters wore white shirts with big red sashes around their full middles and black trousers. The river smelled clean and cool and Anna thought how much fun it would be to spend an evening here.

Then she waved the photograph of Stephen Fuller she'd clipped from the newspaper. "Do you remember him talking to anybody in particular?"

The bartender had to think about that a moment. Then he snapped his fingers, making a sound like breaking wood. "The doctor."

"The who?"

He nodded to the end of the bar where a frail, grave man in a dark suit sat alone cracking a hardboiled egg and pouring salt into his beer. "The doctor. We call him that because years ago he went to the University of Iowa to be a doctor but he ran out of money and now he works as an assistant at the livery. But he likes it when we call him the doctor."

Breathlessly, already starting to push her way through the crowd, she thanked the bartender and went up to the man called "the doctor."

She nudged his shoulder and said, "I understand you were talking to this man earlier."

He glanced up. "Hmmm. You're wearing a badge."

"Yes," she said impatiently. She waved the newspaper clipping again. "You were talking to this man?"

He pointed to his eyes. "Sorry. Bad eyesight. Just a minute."

With frail arthritic hands he took from the interior of his rumpled dark suit coat a pair of wire-rimmed specs. Seeing how gnarled his hands were, she felt ashamed that she'd allowed her impatience to make her so rude.

He put on the specs and then looked at the clipping. "Fuller," he said. He seemed to be in his late fifies, gaunt, with a huge nose and papery skin. What little black hair he had was slicked back almost like a skull-cap. She had seldom seen a man look more alone.

"Yes, Fuller," she said, trying to sound cordial and polite.

"Nice man."

"Yes."

"Bought me three rounds."

"That was nice of him."

"You're looking for him."

"Yes."

"With your badge." A shrewdness came into his eyes.

"Not to arrest him. To help him." There was a defensive note in her voice. She was losing some of the authority she wanted as a constable. "Was he drunk?"

"Nope. In fact, he wasn't even drinking."

"He wasn't?" She was unable to keep the surprise from her voice.

The doctor kept his steady, grave gaze on her. "Not when he was here, anyway. But I wouldn't bet that he lasted long."

"You wouldn't?"

"Saw his hands."

"His hands?"

"The way they trembled. He told me about seeing a friend of his who was dying. My business—over at the livery—I see living creatures die every day. The funny thing is, no matter how long you work at it, you never get used to it."

"Where did he go?"

"That I can't help you with." Then he thought a moment. "Well, now, wait a second. I guess I did mention Malley's. He asked where there was a nice 'civilized' place." The doctor chuckled to himself. "Now there's a nice word, isn't it, 'civilized'?" His eyes narrowed again. "If I was you, I'd try Malley's."

She was getting ready for the push to Malley's. "Thank you, doctor. Thank you."

"Say," he said, smiling at her. "The way you look right now, you might be a little sweet on him, too." He nodded to her badge. "In addition to being a constable, I mean."

She was glad the shadows were so deep here. She could convince herself that the doctor could not see her blush.

Less than a minute later she was on her Imperial and headed for Malley's.

SIXTEEN

He could feel them staring at him and he had absolutely no idea what to do.

The natural thing, of course—if the stories about him were to be believed—was that he would draw his Navy Colt and shoot dead the drunken man who had called him a liar and thrown the drink in his face.

But Stephen Fuller knew his own secret.

That he was, in fact, and indeed, a liar.

Wyatt Earp.

Jesse James.

The Dalton Gang.

During the heyday of those people, Fuller had been a deputy sheriff in a small Oklahoma town where the fiercest thing he had ever faced was a sixteen-year-old boy who'd smashed out a new plate glass window in the general store that he felt had cheated him out of half his paycheck.

The real killings came later and they had been old and drunken men, almost all of them, recalling a romantic era when they had been terrifying men. But they had not been terrifying by the time Fuller as a lawman had gotten them—

"D'you hear me?" the man was shouting. "I say you're a liar!"

Wiping the last of the whiskey away, Fuller, keeping his hand reflexively on his Colt, said, "Gentlemen, I would remove this man for his own sake." What surprised Fuller was the resonance of his voice. The stout stage presence, even in the face of this kind of challenge, remained.

"That's right," said one of the drummers who'd come down the bar. "Why don't we walk down the street to another tavern?" He put his hand on the drunken man's arm. "Come on, now. You're too soused to know what you're doing."

"He didn't know Earp or any of them."

"That's what you say," the drummer said. "But he says different."

"I don't care what he says."

"You gonna gun him, Mr. Fuller?" asked a young businessman almost as drunk as Parsons.

Fuller sighed. "No, I'm not gonna gun him."

And he saw instantly, as he glanced about, that this small crowd was disappointed in exactly the same way as they'd have been if the county fair sword-swallower had announced that he would not be performing tonight.

There was not going to be any show.

"But he threw whiskey in your—"

"I know what he did," Fuller said. He felt old and ashamed and very, very tired. He wanted to go back to Mrs. Goldman's and lie on the bed. Maybe the young constable would come and visit him. He had been thinking a great deal of her blue eyes. Of the melancholy shadow he saw there. Perhaps—

"He's a fraud, that's why."

Fuller slapped him.

He did not even think about it.

One moment he was standing there with his hand on the Navy Colt and the next moment the back of his hand had shot out and caught Parsons clean in the mouth.

The man staggered backwards, thick red blood seeping from his upper lip. His teeth were discolored with blood.

To the drummers, Fuller said, "I asked you once." He nodded to the door. "Get him out of here."

"You bet, Mr. Fuller," the second drummer said, seeing that Fuller was getting angry. "You bet."

Fuller turned away from them completely then, even as Parsons began shouting obscene names.

"I want a shot," Fuller said to the bartender.

"Yessir. And I'd like to thank you."

"For what?"

"For not shooting him in my place. Blood's a sorrowful mess to clean up."

"You're welcome," Fuller said.

The bartender took down a bottle he obviously cherished. "This is the very best stuff I've got."

"Good. I appreciate it."

Lifting the drink, trying not to think of the double XXs he always put on the calendar for a real bender, he hefted the sipping whiskey and threw it back and put down his glass.

The bartender laughed. "Yessir, Mr. Fuller, blood's just sorrowful to clean up, so you go ahead and ask for all the whiskey you want."

By now the other men had gathered around him again and were laughing and slapping him on the back and offering rounds of drinks.

"You ever know John Wesley Hardin?" a man in a straw boater said.

They wanted the stories again, the old good ones, the ones made of whole cloth and spun with loving care with not a single damn word of truth in them.

They wanted the stories again and for a brief bright moment, Fuller looked forward to telling them.

But then, standing there and catching his reflection in the mirror behind three rows of liquor bottles, he saw the older man he was becoming, and he felt a sadness that rocked him certainly as a fist would have.

Suddenly he wanted neither their adulation nor their friendship. He just wanted the clean air of the starry night, and to think through as rationally as he could the nightmare about the orphanage that had lately been troubling his sleep so much.

Without a word, he set down his shot glass and walked out the door.

Parsons let the two drummers take him to a tavern down the street and then he immediately pretended to need a latrine.

Where he went of course was out the back door and down the alley to the tavern from which they'd just come, his hand wrapped tightly around the handle of the big six-shot he kept stuffed into his belt at all times.

He had not forgotten the slap. A man with ten thousand dollars cash in his pocket should not have to tolerate a slap from a has-been gunslinger.

He should not have to tolerate it at all.

It all reminded James Eyles of the Nick Carter yellowbacks Mother had always been taking from him (along with French postcards, his brochure from a company in Cincinnati that taught you to become an undertaker, and the straight razor he sometimes cut himself with when she would not let him out of the cellar).

He had stood across the street in the shadows of a millinery doorway, watching the interior of the tavern where Parsons not only got drunk but threw a drink in the face of some man.

Then he had slipped down the boardwalk, the overhead electric lights, making his progress somewhat risky, following the two drummers as they carried the noisy and flailing Parsons along.

Yes, this was just the sort of thing Nick Carter would have done. All James needed was some kind of disguise but, given his girth, no matter what he did he was going to get noticed.

Next, he stood in the shadows of a wholesale grocery. The night smelled of the dusty street and horse manure and the luxurious chill aroma of nature turning spring green.

He kept his eyes fixed on the shape of Parsons at the bar. As soon as the man tottered to the rear of the tavern, James Eyles sensed something wrong.

He crossed the street, tripping stupidly on the trolley tracks, and then worked his way around to the alley in back.

He wasn't sure why but he had this sense that Parsons was not merely going to the bathroom.

He touched his father's gun reverently as he moved around to the alley.

In the moonlight he could see three empty cargo wagons and the deep shadows of a loading dock. Directly behind the tavern were garbage cans. A tabby cat toyed with something it had dragged from one of the cans. The back door of the tavern squeaked as it opened and there suddenly, still tottering, was Parsons.

James Eyles's first impulse was to shoot him right there. The rage was so overpowering he could scarcely control himself. He never understood the rage or even questioned it, really. He just accepted it the way other people did freckles or a limp. He would be just fine and then a flash of light would appear before his eyes and then this ceaseless need to destroy someone would overcome him.

As it was doing now.

He followed Parsons down the alley.

They went past a small fenced corral where two horses stood, the moonlight outlining them in silver.

They went past a loading platform for the druggist that smelled of turpentine.

They went past the rear of a pool hall where cigar smoke muffled somewhat the clack of balls.

Then they were at an intersection in the alley and he saw what Parsons was going to do.

He was going to sneak back into the tavern where he'd thrown the drink in the man's face.

Parsons took out his gun.

The thing was, Stephen Fuller had no idea if the nightmare were true or not.

He thought it was, anyway—was almost sure of it. But he certainly couldn't have proved it in a court of law.

The nightmare went this way: one night in the orphanage, when Fuller had been no more than five years old, there had been a great clamor in the vestibule downstairs. Awakened by the clamor, and in his nightshirt, the small boy had crept to the edge of the stairs and looked down to see a drunken, painted woman screaming that she was here to see her son. Even then he'd known what her painted face had signified, what kind of woman she was. Then he realized that the name she screamed over and over was his. And that this woman, so ugly in her grief, so tormented in her drunkenness, was his mother.

In the morning a constable in his fine blue uniform had come to the orphanage as the boys and girls were eating breakfast. He had spoken in whispers to Mrs. Emory, who in turn pointed to Stephen. Then both Mrs. Emory and the constable had shaken their heads in pity.

Later that night he had heard Mrs. Emory talking with one of the workers at the orphanage about how the street woman who'd come here drunkenly last night had been found hanging in her cheap little room down off the west end of the tracks.

And now he dreamed of her as she'd been that night—a pretty woman made ugly by too much makeup and too much alcohol.

He wondered why she'd so suddenly shown up to see him and wondered why she'd so suddenly hanged herself in a shabby room in the worst section of town.

He also wondered who his father had been, and why she'd given up young Stephen in the first place.

Questions he would never have resolved . . .

"Fuller!"

Fuller had been so caught up in his thoughts of his mother that he did not even hear the voice in the shadowy depths of the alley.

Only when the gunfire roared between the two story brick buildings did he turn, spinning, his Colt flying on the tips of his fingers from his holster.

He had just enough time to adjust his eyes to the gloom, to see that the man he'd slapped earlier, was falling to the dusty alley in the aftermath of the gunshot.

But Fuller had not fired. . . .

He ran forward to see if the man might simply have drunkenly fired the gun and then toppled over.

He went deep into the alley, thinking that he heard retreating footsteps down another leg of the narrow alleyway.

When he reached Parsons he found two things: a dead man and a fancy gun lying nearby.

He leaned closer to look at the back of the man's coat. Blood sopped the material. Backshot. . . . He thought again of the retreating footsteps he'd heard.

He rolled Parsons over to see if the man might show even a dim sign of life. He touched a finger to the neck and the wrist but nothing. Nothing at all. In the shadows he stared at the dead man. Even in death his face showed a kind of cunning, small desperate dreams come to no good end. He felt a certain pity for Parsons.

Then his eyes fell to the silver revolver near the body and for the first time, Fuller realized there were two guns. The one Parsons held in his hand and this second gun that had apparently been dropped next to the body by the man who'd shot him. . . .

He picked up the silver gun to look at it and it was just then that people from the tavern began flooding into the alley.

"Look!" someone carrying a lantern shouted. "It's Fuller. He's shot the drunk!"

Within moments, a dozen men, several bearing lanterns, encircled Fuller. Still kneeling by the dead man, Fuller felt like a young boy staring up at a group of giant adults.

A drunken face that could not hide its delight in this moment of excitement, leaned down along with a lantern and said, "You'd better be handing your gun over now, Fuller."

To prove his point, the man took out a revolver of his own and put it in Fuller's face.

"You backshot him," the man said, easing the safety off his revolver. "And that means you murdered him."

From the back of the group came a woman's voice, breathless and disturbed.

Anna Tolan reached Fuller and Parsons's body moments later.

Seeing what had happened, or what apparently had happened, she reached over and took from the drunken man his gun and then took her turn at pointing it in Fuller's face.

"I want you to get up now, Mr. Fuller, because I'm placing you under arrest."

SEVENTEEN

Most evenings, done with washing her pinafore for the next morning, Anna liked to sit in the parlor of Mrs. Goldman's and read magazine articles about the famous French detective Marie-Francois Goron. He was a most unlikely hero, being squat and quite overweight, with pince-nez, an asthmatic wheeze, and a rather silly-looking waxed mustache, but as a detective the Chief of the Sûreté was without peer—not only in France but in the world.

Goron had brought both deductive logic and the art of autopsy into play. His most famous case thus far had taken place in 1887 when he solved the murder of a man whose body had been found rotting in a sack near a riverbank. Goron was assigned to the case and, working closely with doctors of various types, pioneer work was done in a method called "autopsy," which helped identify the victim and also determine the manner in which he'd been killed. But this particular murder, even with all the doctors and much of the Paris police department involved, was not easy to solve. Which was why Goron brought to bear another tactic he had refined, if not invented—the process of interrogation. Goron went all over Paris, questioning anybody he felt could bring any valuable information to the case. All he really had to go on was a corpse that had been left to deteriorate for well over a year. Then one day he caught a cab driver in a lie and the whole case came clear to him, the real guilty party (the Paris police had rushed to arrest three innocent men) finally arrested.

Anna had always daydreamed about being presented her first case and solving it in the way Goron would—through medical detective work and shrewd interrogation.

But, presented with such a moment, she found her reactions to the actual situation very different.

For one thing there was the corpse. By now its back was soggy with blood and it smelled, even on this chilly night.

For another there was the small crowd. The lanterns they held cast shadows huge and menacing against the brick wall on the east side of the alley—they put her in mind of the lynch mobs constables feared so much.

And finally there was Stephen Fuller himself. Half-drunk, dazed, he stood next to her like a shamed little boy.

She repeated, "I'm going to have to arrest you."

He barely whispered, "I know."

"He shot him all right, Miss. No doubt about that," said someone from the crowd, a cheeky man in a brown tweed suit.

She decided to apply a little Goron. She stepped up to the cheeky man. "You saw this man—" and here she pointed to Fuller—"shoot this man?" And here she pointed to the corpse.

"Well," said the man. "No. Not exactly, I mean."

"What exactly did you see?"

"Well, I—"

"We saw him standing over him," offered another man. "And it was obvious."

Now she turned her attention to the tall man whom she recognized as a haberdasher over on Second Avenue. "What was obvious?" she said.

"That Fuller here shot the man."

"What made it obvious?"

"Well, he was standing over him."

"Did he have a gun in his hand?"

"Yes."

"Which gun?"

"The one you've got in your hand."

"This one?" She showed the silver revolver.

"Yes."

She held the gun even higher in the thick yellow lantern light. "Anybody else see Fuller with this gun in his hand?"

Three other men spoke up right away, agreeing that they had indeed seen Fuller with the gun.

"He's the killer, no doubt about that," a bald man said. "I was in the tavern when the dead man there threw a drink in Fuller's face and called him a liar."

Anna heard this news with a sense that she was smothering in a bad dream.

She kept staring at Fuller and wanting to believe that somehow he was innocent.

But there was the gun he'd been seen holding and now— and here was one of Goron's other obsessions—now there was motive. The dead man had insulted him.

Calmly, she said, "Now I want you to listen very carefully to my next question."

The men began glancing at each other there in the alley, their heads plump with bowlers and derbies, their mouths packed with the stubs of cigars and the curve of the long-stemmed German pipes popular the past few years, the lantern light continuing to flicker across their faces.

"You sure you should be doing this, Anna?" a man asked.

"I'm a constable," Anna said. She wished her voice hadn't sounded quite so defensive.

"Technically, Anna," said the haberdasher, "you're a police matron." He was careful not to sound unkind.

"Well," Anna said, "since I'm the only one here wearing a badge, I think I'll just put myself in charge for a few minutes."

"How about if I go get a real—" The bald man stopped. "Get a regular constable."

Anna frowned. "A man, in other words."

"Just a regular constable, Anna. No reason you should take offense," the haberdasher said.

Anna sighed. "All right. But before you go, I want you to

answer my question." She pointed to Fuller. "Now several of you will testify that you saw Stephen Fuller standing over the dead man with this silver revolver in his hand, correct?"

"Yes," said several men.

"Did any of you actually see him shoot the man?"

"Now, Anna, what kind of question is that?" asked the haberdasher. "It stands to reason that if he was standing over the dead man with a gun in his hand, he was the one who shot him."

The haberdasher looked around at the other men for confirmation of his point. Several men grumbled agreement.

"Then none of you actually saw Fuller shoot the man?"

"Oh, Anna," the haberdasher said, as if he were frustrated with a very young and stupid girl. "Why don't you leave the detective work to your boy friend David Peary?"

Anna flushed, and for two reasons. One, she felt quite capable of handling the case herself (that was how Goron always referred to detective matters, as "cases"). And two, had the entire town of Cedar Rapids gone and gotten her married off to Detective David Peary?

"I'm repeating my question one more time," Anna said. "Did any of you actually see Fuller shoot the man on the ground?"

"Well," said the haberdasher, "if you're going to get technical, no, we didn't actually see Fuller here shoot the man— but who else would have done it?"

Anna nodded to the haberdasher. "Why don't you run off and get a *real* constable now?"

"It's not like you to hold a grudge," the man said just before taking off in a long-legged lope out of the alley and down the street.

Anna knelt next to the dead man. The first thing Goron did when coming upon a corpse was to clean out his pockets. "Murder victims often hold the identity of their killers right on their bodies," Goron had been quoted as saying recently.

The pants pockets, where she began, turned up nothing more than some change, a comb, a plug of tobacco, some candy meant to sweeten the breath, and the stub end of a train ticket.

"Shoot," she said.

She glanced up at Fuller. He looked lost and confused as ever. He was obviously coming sober, and coming sober fast, and all this would have the claustrophobic air of a nightmare to him.

Fuller said to her, "I didn't shoot him. I really didn't."

She offered him an expression meant to cheer him up a bit but she didn't dare offer him a real smile. Not in front of these men.

She returned to searching the dead man, this time his suit coat. The smell was very bad because the gunshot wound was still pumping blood and because the man's bowels had not held.

The right interior pocket held nothing but the card of a tailor. It noted the tailor's name and the day the suit had been sold—today, in fact, only a few hours ago. The card guaranteed the owner the right to bring the suit back for free alterations anytime within a thirty-day period from the date on the card.

Anna tucked the card in the pocket of her pinafore.

She next went to work on the left interior pocket. She did not have to work long. She pulled from the pocket a long white business envelope. It was plump and its contents had almost sharp edges. She knew at once what she was feeling.

Money.

She glanced up at the curious crowd watching her. To them she offered the same elusive sort of expression she'd just visited on Fuller.

Without a word, or without even looking at the envelope, she took it and pushed it into the pocket of her pinafore along with the tailor's card.

She was just standing up—and was therefore off-balance—when Stephen Fuller made his move.

He grabbed the silver revolver from her hand and then spun toward the crowd.

Quietly, he said, "Now I'm going to walk backwards to the

end of this alley and not a one of you is going to make a move. Is that understood?"

Clearly aware of his reputation—and obviously convinced that Fuller had just shot the man on the ground—the crowd rumbled its compliance.

"I didn't kill this man," Fuller said, still not raising his voice, "but every one of you seems to think I did so there isn't much I can do about it."

"This isn't the right thing to do," Anna said.

"Maybe not," Fuller said. "But neither is waiting in a jail for a jury to find me guilty for something I didn't do."

"If you're innocent, I'll help find who actually killed him. Have you ever heard of Goron?"

She saw instantly that it was the wrong thing to say.

There had been an almost social note to her words and here was a man desperate as an animal—sweaty now and hollow-eyed in the lurid yellow lantern light.

He was in no mood to hear about some pudgy little French detective named Goron.

He eased the safety off the revolver and said, "Remember now, I'm moving down the alley and right now I don't have a damn thing to lose. Not a damn thing."

Once again the small crowd nodded its compliance.

In less than a minute, Stephen Fuller had walked down the alley backwards and vanished from sight.

EIGHTEEN

On that spring night the following events occurred in Cedar Rapids: There was a pavilion dance at the Cedar Springs Hotel, a man named George O. Williams (graduate of Trinity College, London, England) gave his first piano lesson here; Karl Stevenson (an eleven-year-old boy) lugging home a block from Hubbard Ice dropped same on his toe and broke both block and his big toe (right foot); a young socialite named Miss Louise Baker gave a game of progressive hearts for other young socialites; the *Cedar Rapids Evening Gazette* apologized to the Reverend Doctor Tilden for giving the wrong title to his sermon (the real title being "Fidelity and Her Crown," the *Gazette* compositor had made it "Infidelity and Her Crown," which had been worth more than a few laughs); Cedar Rapids pounded Waterloo in a baseball game 10 to 3; a visiting Utah politician named Reynolds bitterly described the effects of the mining collapse in his home state and urged Republicans everywhere to fight for the silver standard; "cigarette fiends" were invited to take the "brand new 1893 stop smoking course" offered by one C. H. French; Jones the Dentist was offering "the very best set of life-like teeth for only $8.00"; Albert L. Hromatko, aged nineteen, died at the home of his parents of complications following influenza; Ford's Turkish Baths found itself with an overflow crowd; and on the second floor of the Cedar Rapids Constabulary a young woman named Anna Tolan found herself facing a very angry chief named Ryan.

"You should've sent for another constable right away."

"You mean a man."

"All right, then, Anna, I mean a man."

"He didn't seem dangerous."

"He'd just committed a murder and he didn't seem dangerous?"

"I don't believe he killed that man, Chief Ryan."

"You don't believe he killed that man?"

"No."

"And just what leads you to that brilliant conclusion?"

"He said he didn't."

"He said he didn't. Now there's a persuasive piece of work."

"If you'd have seen his face, you'd know what I was talking about."

"The man had called him a liar, hadn't he?"

"Yes."

"Then thrown a drink in his face?"

"Yes."

"And Fuller was seen in the alley with the dead man?"

"Yes."

"And Fuller was holding a weapon, presumably the murder weapon?"

"Presumably."

"But he didn't do it?"

"No. I don't believe he did."

Chief Ryan, who still had white wisps of talcum powder on his face from shaving (being one of those men who had to shave twice a day), sat back, lit his pipe, and looked at Anna. "This has to do with that Goron business, doesn't it?"

"Well . . ."

"Answer me, Anna."

"Well, Goron always says to 'discount the obvious.' "

"The obvious being that a drunken man, with a record of violence, is seen by at least a dozen witnesses standing in the alley over his victim with the murder weapon—and we're supposed to discount that."

Softly, she said, "I think we should look around for other explanations."

Just then she heard footsteps coming up the stairs outside. The creak of leather shoes. The odor of cigarette smoke. The scent of bay rum after-shave.

David Peary, dapper as always, leaned into the chief's office and said, "Two of our men spotted Fuller running along the river near the ice houses."

"They're closing in?"

"They should be."

"Good."

Peary looked at Anna. "Is she telling you about Goron?"

"Yes."

Anna had expected a sarcastic remark backing up the chief's skepticism. Instead, David Peary said, "You know something, Chief?"

"What?"

"In most cases, I agree with her about Goron."

"That little Frenchman?"

Peary nodded. "What he's doing with interrogation techniques and medical science is really astonishing."

"Then you think Fuller is innocent?"

Peary glanced at Anna. He looked almost afraid to speak. He said, "No, I'm afraid Anna's wrong in this case. I think we've got the right man." He paused. "And I think Anna should not have tried to act like a constable but remembered that she is, after all, a matron."

The chief, seeing for himself Anna's mood, said, "Well, if nothing else I know I got a very thorough investigation at the crime scene."

"How's that?" Peary said.

"Tell him, Anna."

Anna said, "The footprints."

The chief coughed on his pipe and said, "More of that damn scientific stuff. Pardon my French."

"What footprints?" Peary asked.

Anna went over and sat on the edge of the chief's desk. The lithograph of George Washington watched her with paternal severity. "Leading to the body all the way down to the opposite end of the alley and then down the block. Muddy prints."

"Muddy?" Peary said. "It hasn't rained in four days."

"That's my point. Where would muddy prints come from if it hadn't rained in four days?"

"She does have an interesting point, Chief."

"Interesting or just diverting?" the chief asked. "Do you really think this makes Fuller any less than our number one suspect?"

"Not at all," Peary said confidently. "I would wager that if we inspected his boots, we'd find some sort of mud on them."

Anna, hearing this, sighed. She had never considered the possibility that the mysteriously muddy prints might have belonged to Stephen Fuller.

"Did you check Fuller's feet, Anna?" Peary asked.

"Well, no, in the rush I—"

"There you go," Peary said, turning back to the chief. "That should be the clincher."

"What should?" the chief asked.

"As soon as Bannion and Malley bring him in, we'll check his feet. Then we'll have witnesses who saw him standing over the body, we'll have the murder weapon he used, and now we'll have the boots that made the muddy footprints. Carlson will love us." Carlson was the county attorney.

"Well," Chief Ryan said. "I guess that would make for an even better case."

Peary winked at Anna. "All thanks to the Goron method of detective work." He pulled out his Elgin pocket watch and ceremoniously consulted it. "I'd say Bannion and Malley should be along anytime now."

And, as if on cue, they heard from the lobby downstairs the tramping feet of at least two men rushing up the stairs.

Peary smiled, obviously taking pride in the swift way his men had apprehended Stephen Fuller.

Malley, a thickset man in blue uniform, was so out of breath he nearly fell through the doorway.

He looked at his immediate superior, Peary, instead of the chief. "You won't believe it."

"Believe what?" Peary said, already sounding tense.

"He got away. We chased him all the way down the river to the bridge and he just got clean away."

"Damn," David Peary said. "Damn." Then he glanced at Anna. "Pardon my French, Anna."

Chief Ryan said, with more melancholy than anger, "You should have called for a man to back you up sooner, Anna. Then he wouldn't have got away."

Anna nodded. For the first time she agreed with the chief—even though her mind was still filled with the image of Stephen Fuller's sad and confused gaze. "I guess I should have," she said, not feeling like a real constable at all now. "I guess I should have at that."

NINETEEN

Mother would not have been happy.

James Eyles stood in the kitchen looking at the mud he'd brought in on his shoes.

At first the dirty tracks confused him. Where could they have come from?

Gulping, he remembered.

Mother had been working on her spring flower bed all day, using manure and water in the rich Iowa soil. She'd used so much water that a large area of the backyard had been soaked.

He could recall the squishy feeling from the ground in which he'd buried her. Now he began wondering how good a grave it was, made up mainly of mud.

Wandering dogs would have no trouble. . . .

He went upstairs. From the linen closet he brought a clean fluffy new white towel, and from a secret drawer in his bureau he brought three especially nice French postcards, and from a humidor in his father's den he took one of the plump Cuban cigars his mother hated so much.

He was still shaking from killing Parsons. Sometimes, following a killing, he would vomit. Other times he would get terrible headaches. And sometimes there was just a gnawing anxiety that no amount of liquor could help.

Usually baths helped.

He would lie in bathwater hot as he could stand and smoke a cigar and look at French postcards and eventually the fear would go away.

He moved through the vast, shadowy, museum-like house, a bronze bust of Shakespeare in one corner of the second floor, a gigantic reproduction of a Vermeer painting in the other.

Ten minutes later, the tub filled and steaming, he eased himself into the water.

It was so hot on his plump flesh that he went "ooo" and "ouch" and "gosh" and (Mother hated swearing) "shoot" as he forced himself into what seemed to be burning flames.

Then, finally, his wide bottom touched the bottom of the tub and he sat there for several minutes adjusting to the searing heat of the water until—

—until, sweat pouring off him in a wonderful cleaning-out process, he began to enjoy himself.

Oh, yes, he was going to feel much better about it all in the morning.

Much better.

He lit the cigar and leaned his head back against the wide curving rear lip of the bathtub and closed his eyes.

He thought of Paris in spring. Glimpses of women he knew to be prostitutes paraded past his eyes. He smelled the warm, flower-laden Parisian nights and saw the Seine as midnight lanterns burnished its smooth dark surface. Paris was no place to be for a young man burdened with Mother. No place at all.

He leaned over and picked up the French postcards.

He stayed in the tub an hour and a half, as the water went from hot to warm to downright chilly.

Finished with his postcards and his cigar, exhausted now and wanting only to roll into his own bed with its fresh sheets and plump pillows, he started to pull himself from the tub when he heard the noise.

Mother always said he had "too much imagination." As a youngster he was forever waking up in the middle of the night and crying out for her to come save him from the demons and goblins that had invaded his bedroom.

Suddenly, as he wrapped the towel around his considerable middle, he felt the same kind of numbing fear he'd known as a youngster.

Only this time it wasn't demons and goblins that frightened him.

This time it was the possibility of the constables coming and saying *we know what you did* and taking him off to a place much worse than Mother's cellar had been.

He thought: *All I want to do is get to Paris and spend the rest of my life there. I promise I will never hurt anyone again. I promise.*

He hadn't thought about it but he supposed he was praying.

From downstairs came the sounds that had alarmed him a few moments ago.

Someone, definitely, was in the house.

Within his fleshy chest his heart was like a wild bird. Within the darkness of his mind he saw with the clarity of a nickelodeon image a constable in blue bearing a badge and a gun.

He would be arrested. . . .

He moved as quickly as possible, leaving the bathroom and sneaking down the shadowed hallway to his bedroom.

He closed the door, yanked a Queen Anne chair from next to his reading table, and shoved it up under the knob so no one could get through.

He pulled on a nightshirt, picked up a baseball bat he'd kept from childhood in the corner, and then turned out the lamp.

Footsteps on the winding stairway now. Definitely.

The whole soul of the house seemed to creak and groan with the weight of this intruder.

Standing in the corner, painted in silver moonlight and looking like a comic statue, James stood with the ball bat at the ready for whomever came through that door.

The hallway boards creaked now.

Closer. Coming closer.

James, clutching the bat, felt as if he might suffocate.

Who could it be? Who, other than the authorities, knew his secret and was coming to get him?

A hand on the doorknob. Turning it sharply leftward. Then sharply rightward.

James, holding the bat aloft. Prepared.

The knob was rattled now, as if a giant creature meant to tear it from the door itself.

My God, James thought. My God.

And then the most incredible sound of all.

He stood there, scarcely breathing, astonished at the noise that had just echoed through the high gilt ceilings of this sprawling mansion.

There had been a time, during those years when he'd been prone to hives and bed-wetting, when his dreams had been so real that they never quite left him, even during the daylight hours. He would walk around having conversations with the people in his head and no amount of stern discouragement could bring him fully into reality.

He felt like that now.

What he'd just heard was impossible, of course.

Impossible.

He held the bat the way a player would who was about ready to hit a home run.

The door knob was again rattled with relentless violence.

And once again the sound was made.

The impossible sound.

Footsteps retreating—and James's heart a dying beast within him.

Footsteps gathering momentum and running toward the bedroom door and—

The crash was impressive, ripping wood from wood, slamming the slab of door back against the wall.

And then in the moonlight the impossible sound once again, only this time he knew it was real, for there she stood, right in front of him, hands on hips, angry as always, screeching as always.

"James!" cried Mother. "You put that vulgar bat down and help me wash the blood off my head!"

TWENTY

Anna was just going up Mrs. Goldman's front steps, when the pebble landed against one of the round white pillars supporting the porch.

Startled, she turned, letting her gaze search quickly through the deep gloom surrounding the house. The pebble seemed to have come from somewhere near the hedges running eastward along the periphery of the lawn.

A second pebble landed in approximately the same spot on the pillar.

Following this one, and before Anna had time to flee, a slender male figure emerged from the darkness, coming into a patch of moonlit silver on the dewy grass.

"I wanted to catch your attention before you went in," Stephen Fuller said, tipping his hat in a curiously formal way.

"You scared me," she said.

"Anybody up?" he asked, nodding to the house.

Nobody appeared to be. Interior darkness pressed the lace curtains. The scents of supper—Mrs. Goldman's "famous Yiddish spaghetti" as she liked to call it—mixed pleasantly with the exterior smells of dogwood trees and the new earth.

He nodded once again to the porch. "Thought maybe we could sit up there on the swing and talk."

"I'm not sure that would be a good idea, Mr. Fuller."

"So I'm still 'Mister,' eh?"

She could see that her tone—cold, official—was hurting him. But she didn't know how else to act. She was very conscious, suddenly, of being a constable, one who had been derelict in her duty. "You should never have run away," she said. Her voice was a bit gentler now.

"It was starting to look too easy."

"Too easy?"

"Right. For the authorities. For the jury. For the judge. There I was standing in the alley with a man who'd insulted me not twenty minutes before." He looked at her out of narrowed eyes. "Way too easy. And I wouldn't stand a chance."

At first she'd thought he was angry but now, once more, she sensed that there was more pain than anger in the man.

"Then you didn't kill him?"

"No."

She paused a moment. "Do you promise me that?"

"Promise you?"

"Yes."

"You mean like taking an oath?"

"Exactly. Swearing on the thing you hold most holy in all the world."

Now it was his turn to pause. "I guess that would be my feelings for Boyd Haskell. He's like my brother."

"Then do you swear on your feelings for Boyd Haskell that you didn't kill that man tonight?"

"I swear."

Her sigh was audible.

"You sound mighty relieved," he said. There was a hint of humor in his voice.

"I *am* mighty relieved."

"Well, I appreciate that. Believing me, I mean."

Her next sigh had a different quality. A note of despair. "They're looking for you. Chief Ryan's calling everybody in tonight, even the auxiliary men."

Glumly, he said, "Maybe I should just turn myself in." Now it was his turn to sigh. "I'm too tired to run." He shrugged. "Maybe I'm too old to run."

"You're not an old man," she said.

"No, but I'm a weary one."

The night was noisy with dogs suddenly, yipping, barking, snapping dogs.

Down the middle of the wide dirt street in front of Mrs. Goldman's came three lawmen, two of whom held onto the leashes of four bloodhounds.

The dogs were so eager, they jerked and tugged the constables along without the men having much control at all.

Anna and Fuller glanced at each other. Anna knew she would have to make a decision right here and now. She had the terrible sense that no matter what her decision was, she would somehow come to regret it.

She raised her eyes to the garage near the back of the house.

"There's a loft up there you can hide in."

"Are you serious?"

"Just go hide."

"But your job—"

She might have been addressing a child. "You heard me. Go hide in the loft. I'll go out to the street and see what's going on."

"But—"

"Hurry."

David Peary and his lamp came a few feet behind the constables being dragged along by the bloodhounds in front of Mrs. Goldman's.

In the constabulary some of the younger constables liked to joke about what they liked to call Detective Peary's "head lamp," but to Peary the Ferguson Universal Reflecting Lamp, which rode on the front brim of his derby (thanks to the Ferguson's patented head strap) was no laughing matter. With its silver-plated locomotive reflector, the lamp could illuminate objects as far away as sixty feet, and "shine" an animal's eyes from a hundred-yard distance. What's more, it burned oil for up to nine hours, which made it ideal for all-night searches, such as tonight's.

Peary, son of a local banker and a mother whose colorful brother was chief constable in Reading, Pennsylvania, supposed that to his underlings he probably did look a little funny in his rather strange hat contraption—but then much of what he did the other constables found funny.

Peary had spent two years after college in Chicago studying the methods of criminology as practiced by such diverse men as Alan Pinkerton, Alphonse Bertillon, and Anna Tolan's favorite, Goron. He had also delved extensively into the work of such men as Cesare Bonesana, who wrote the first book on criminology in 1764, and which proposed that criminals could be reformed only through uniform application of laws, speedy trials, and humane treatment. Bloody punishments, sometimes for even minor infractions, did not rehabilitate the criminal at all, Bonesana argued. More recently—and this had been strongly argued among the young constables taking criminology classes—there was a new and popular theory that was threatening to supersede Beccaria's notion that criminals weren't born but were rather produced by adverse social conditions. The new belief was espoused by a contemporary Italian physician named Cesare Lombroso, who believed that the criminal could be studied scientifically, much in the fashion Goron proposed, and that only through careful and objective analysis of a crime scene could the facts be arrived at justly. The most controversial part of Lombroso's theory had to do with the "looks" of a criminal, the doctor believing that criminals shared certain physical traits that made them different from other people. Over schooners of beer at a student tavern near the Northwestern campus, nothing was more fun to argue over than Lombroso.

"The dogs seem pretty agitated," one of the constables said over his shoulder to Peary.

Peary turned his head from side to side, letting his Ferguson Universal Reflecting Lamp shine into various corners of the Goldman lawn.

Though he saw nothing untoward, he did share the constable's curiosity about the sudden agitation of the brown and white hounds.

Suddenly, from the gloom, he saw the one person who could cause him to lose the control he so prided himself on— Anna Tolan, of course.

Still garbed in her pinafore and wearing her badge, she swept down from the porch and along the paved walk and out to the street where the uniformed constables were holding tight to the jerking and twisting hounds.

"Good evening, Anna," Peary said, trying to keep his voice down to its usual baritone level. Sometimes when he saw Anna, his voice inadvertently rose an octave or two and he sounded like a very young boy.

She seemed as agitated as the dogs. "No luck yet?" she asked.

"Not yet."

She appeared to be perspiring a great deal and she could not quite meet his eyes. "Well, I'm sure you'll catch him, David." Her voice, too, seemed an octave or two higher. Strained. She knitted and unknitted her hands. David Peary observed all this carefully, the way in which the masters, Bertillon and Goron, would have.

What was wrong with Anna, particularly when she kept casting anxious glances over her shoulder and back into the gloom surrounding the east side of the large white Victorian house?

Then, at least briefly, she was the old Anna.

"I see you're playing trolley car again," she smiled, and nodded to the Ferguson Universal Reflecting Lamp strapped to his derby.

"It's really very helpful."

"I'm sure it is," Anna said and there was that rare note of affection for David in her voice. "It's just that you look so silly and earnest at the same time—sort of like a very earnest young boy." She touched his elbow gently. "But cute, David. Definitely cute."

The two constables, even above the yipping dogs, obviously heard her words and smiled at each other.

David Peary felt himself flush. Here he'd dreamed for the past three years of Anna saying something at least vaguely romantic like this (at night he hugged and kissed his pillow, imagining it to be Anna dressed in a beautiful spring frock and nodding assent to his proposal of marriage)—and now she had to go and say it in front of two other people, giving him no chance whatsoever to respond.

Peary cleared his throat. "Is everything all right?"

"All right?" Anna said, the anxiety seeming to be back in her voice. "Of course."

"The dogs yipping—very strange."

"Everything's fine. I was just sitting on the porch watching the moon. You know how I like to watch the clouds race past the moon. It's one of the most beautiful sights ever."

"Yes, it is," Peary said. Then he caught the soft, seductive sound of his tone—and imagined the two constables to be smiling again. He stood up straight, in compensation, and touched his derby to make sure that his Ferguson was in place. To them, he said, "Maybe we'd better have a look around Mrs. Goldman's house. The dogs seem disturbed."

"That they do," one of the constables said.

Anna took his arm. "David, really, there's nothing. I walked around the house when I put my Imperial in the garage for the night. Everything's fine. And if the dogs get any closer—" She made a show of shaking her head sorrowfully. "Well, you know how some of Mrs. Goldman's boarders are. If the dogs wake them up, they'll never get back to sleep." She touched his sleeve again. "Let me check things before I go to bed just to be on the safe side and if there's any trouble I'll use my whistle and a constable can come running."

"But the dogs—"

"You know how skittish they are." She smiled. "Remember the night they thought they'd trapped that bank robber in the city barns—and all it turned out to be was a kitten?"

"Well—"

"And that's all they're barking at now. Please, David, let's not wake Mrs. Goldman's boarders."

Peary glanced at the other constables. "Why don't you take them down the block toward the river? I guess that'd be a more likely place."

"But, sir, the dogs—"

"It's probably just a cat or something," Peary said, sounding more confident than he felt. The dogs weren't all *that* skittish, even if they did occasionally make a mistake.

Constables and dogs faded into the patches of darkness beneath the streetlight twenty yards away, one with the gloom now except the muted barking.

Peary felt, despite the occasion being a manhunt, thrilled to be standing here with Anna Tolan. His mind was vivid with images of the house they could live in, the children they could raise, the Sunday buggy drives they could take.

"Anna . . ." he said.

"I'd better go in now," she said. "I'm very tired."

"I just wanted to . . . apologize, I guess."

She looked genuinely surprised. "You, David, apologize? I didn't think you were capable of that?"

"I shouldn't have been so—patronizing back at the chief's office, Anna. You were only doing what you thought was right. You couldn't know that a skunk like Fuller would run away. So, I'm sorry."

Then she did the most wonderful and unheard-of thing of all.

She stood on her toes and leaned up and kissed him on the cheek.

His mind became an electric and whirling entity threatening to go completely out of control.

"Anna, I—"

"I'd better go in now."

"But couldn't we talk a little?"

She smiled at him. It was, curiously, a sad frown. "Not tonight, David. I really am tired."

"But—"

"Maybe we could go for a soda tomorrow after work."

"That would be wonderful, Anna. That would be wonderful." His baritone had gone up two octaves again.

"Goodnight, David," she said, touching his sleeve.

He watched her go up the walk. He stood beneath the moon and the dogwoods and the elms and the oaks, the night quiet but for crickets, and felt as if this moment was a very special piece of time, frozen and immortalized much like a painting.

She had touched him, she had kissed him, she had invited him to invite her for a soda tomorrow.

Yes, this was a very special time and he tried desperately not to ruin it by worrying about two things—why the dogs had barked so passionately and why Anna had seemed so reluctant to have him check out Mrs. Goldman's grounds.

No, he did not want to spoil the moment with his college-trained cynicism.

Tonight belonged to Keats and Shelley and Shakespeare's sonnets (David liked to consider himself a well-rounded man), not to the cold truths of Bertillon and Goron.

He went down the street whistling a sentimental song that Cedar Rapidians liked to sing on certain lazy summer nights at the Greene Opera House.

He whistled, and his Ferguson Universal Reflecting Lamp rode perfectly still on his derby.

TWENTY-ONE

Leave it to Mother, James Eyles thought as he sat in the vast lamp-lit kitchen, stuffing cake into his mouth and her existence into his eyes.

She was still alive.

After at least—or so he recalled in the frenzied memory of it all—eight blows smack across the head, not to mention being buried under four feet of heavy dirt that should have smothered—

Still alive.

And clever. To hide the places where he had hit her, she'd not only cleaned herself up but set upon her head a plump purple turban she'd picked up in a Parisian salon, one of which James had never been unduly fond because it gave her the aspect of a circus swami.

A fresh, dark silk dress covering her bulk, the turban at a slight angle to cover the bandages she'd wrapped about her head, she looked as if she'd just enjoyed another night at home cursing Democrats, doing needlepoint, and questioning James about the girl who worked at Kleven's Grocery (Mother was always fearful that some young tart would steal James away).

It could have been just any other spring night except for the fact that she had (1) been beaten the hell out of (2) thrown in the corner of a cellar as rat food and (3) later been buried alive.

"Now," Mother said, "I want you to tell Mother you're sorry."

"I'm sorry."

"No you're not."

"I am sorry, Mother."

"If you were truly sorry, you wouldn't say it that way. First of all you would come over here and give me a kiss."

"Oh," he said. But he didn't move.

"Well?"

He got up and went around the wide circle of table and put a tight-lipped little kiss on her well-powdered cheek.

"You kiss me as if it's a most unpleasant task," Mother said.

"No, Mother, I like kissing you."

"Then kiss me as if you meant it. Kiss me the way Andre always does."

Andre was the hairdresser whom she occasionally took with them through Europe and upon whom she threw Yankee dollars like leaflets and impatience like knives.

"I never cared much for Andre, Mother."

"And just what's wrong with him?"

"He's strange."

She fixed him a taxidermist's glare and then said, "Good God, you've killed all those people and you say *Andre* is strange?"

"He gushes. Gushing makes me nervous for some reason."

Mother, her turban riding confidently over her bandages, pointed to the big pound cake like a queen pointing an accusatory finger at an uncompliant subject. "Now you sit down there and eat all of that cake and tell me about everybody you've killed."

"I'm not hungry, Mother. I'm sorry."

She shook her head, holding the turban as she did so. "You know you're never really happy unless you're stuffed. Now you sit right down there and eat. Do you hear me?"

He dragged himself back to the chair and sat down and began stuffing the rest of the pound cake into his mouth.

"So," she said, "how many has it been?"

"I'm not sure."

"You're not sure."

"Within one or two I'm certain."

"My Lord."

"There was one in Ohio I drowned but he might have swum to the far shore. I'm not sure."

"My Lord."

"Then there was the one I set fire to in St. Louis."

"You're not sure about somebody you set fire to?"

"He rolled off this cliff to put the fire out." James Eyles shrugged. "He might have survived the fall."

"And all these vile people called you names?"

He had some more cake. "Terrible names."

"Well, I can see where that would set somebody off. Name calling, I have reference to. But me—" Tears were in her voice. "Mother. I'm your dear, protective Mother— Why would you try to kill me?"

"I'm not sure."

"You're not sure?"

"Something just came over me."

"The flash?"

"Something very much like the flash. I'd been playing with a mouse and—"

"Playing with a mouse?"

More cake. Another nod. A big gulp. Then kind of a grin. "Squeezing him."

"Squeezing him?"

He held up a giant hand and made a fist of it. "Squeezing it. Like this." He made the fist even tighter.

For the first time a curious look came into Mother's eyes. He could recall seeing this particular look only one other time

—when a Unitarian had tried to tell her that the words of the Bible were the work of men and not of God. Disbelief had come into her gaze—disbelief and scorn and a kind of profound unpleasantness, as if she had just identified the most discomfiting species of life on the entire planet. "And what happens to the mouse?"

"Happens?"

"Yes, as you're squeezing harder?"

"It pops."

"Pops?"

"Sure. You know. Kind of explodes."

"The mouse explodes?"

"Sure. You can feel its little ribs snapping and then blood and things starting to come from its mouth and—" He was getting heady just talking about it, forgetting all about Mother being here, heady the way he got upstairs in his room with the French postcards and their plump Parisian tarts. . . .

"Please," Mother said. She had become so agitated listening to him that her turban had slid once more. Now an edge of white bandage was revealed beneath the edge of the fancy headpiece. Then she adjusted not only the turban but herself. "In your room upstairs."

This was Mother at her best. She loved to make opening comments like this. Set him on edge, fearful of what to expect. "In your room upstairs" could be the opening part of the vilest sort of accusation and that was just what Mother wanted him to think.

She repeated, "In your room upstairs."

"Yes, Mother."

"Your bags are packed."

"Yes, Mother."

"You thought I was dead and then you were going—where?"

That was another trick of Mother's. To virtually slap you with a single word by putting a long and lacerating pause in front of it, in this case "where" being the important word.

"The continent. France. probably."

"You were going to see our friends in Europe."

He said it too quickly. "Yes. Our friends in Europe."

She pointed to the cake again. "You need some more cake."

"I'm stuffed, Mother. Really."

"I'd think the least favor you could grant me after trying to kill me is to have a little more cake."

He had a little more cake.

As he began to eat, she said, "You weren't going to see our friends, were you?"

"Who else would I see, Mother?" Actually, he said it *moom-elsh-wooood-I-sheee* because his mouth was filled with pound cake.

"Tarts."

"Tarts?"

"Girls like the one at Kleven's Grocery. Streetgirls and shopgirls who want nothing more than your money." She paused. "You know very well what tarts are, James. You have all those postcards of them up in your room."

He felt his face glow red and sweat began to bead on his forehead.

"And I know why you have those postcards, too, don't think I don't."

She let herself fall back in the chair. She looked fat and exhausted and old—very, very old suddenly—and for the first time in his life he felt something like pity for her.

She sat, once more adjusting her turban with plump fingers. "You're not grateful for anything I've ever done for you, are you?"

"I'm very grateful, Mother."

"I look around and see how miserable most men are because of women—that's the ultimate misery a man can know, James. The misery women inflict on men. And here I've unselfishly devoted my life to keeping you from knowing that misery and look at what I get."

She then fell to sobbing in a way he'd never heard her sob.

He had no idea what to do but eat.

He sat there just watching her and filling his mouth until his shirt felt so tight the buttons threatened to burst.

Then, wailing now, her turban slid off completely and there she sat, this huge woman wearing too much pancake makeup, completely bald-looking because of the bandages that covered her skull.

He laughed out loud.

He knew instantly it was the wrong thing to do but he could not help himself. All his life his mother had been such a commanding presence but now—her head swathed in bandages—she looked—

Comic.

She stood up.

She bent to retrieve the turban.

She set the turban aright and then with great dignity came around the table to him.

She slapped him loud as a gunshot.

She slapped him so loud and so hard that he let out a cry that sounded like a woman's.

Then she said, "I am the only living person who knows your secret."

But he was crying himself, now, and scarcely listening.

"I know what a vile, dirty little boy you are. I know what you do up in the privacy of your bedroom and I know what you do to other people when you're traveling alone. How would you like it if I told other people what you do?"

But he could not listen, only cry. Her slap had reclaimed her rightful position as his dominator—she had never ever before in his life slapped him—and now he could only sob as, earlier, she herself had sobbed.

"We're going to Europe, all right, James. But it will be my friends we live with—not your tarts. And you're going to be a good little boy again or I will tell the appropriate people your secrets. And believe me, I'll do that. Because I'd rather have you dead than disobedient. Do you understand me, James?"

A great and final door was closing on James Eyles just then.

A great and final door—far more massive than the cellar

that had imprisoned him all these years—and now there was just darkness and coldness and the dank smell of eternity.

"Do you understand me?" she shouted. "Do you understand me?"

TWENTY-TWO

"What's that?" David Peary said.

He stood, his handsome features looking somewhat pinched from exhaustion, in the doorway to the room the constables used to have coffee.

The time was the following morning, 10:30 A.M. Chief Ryan, having pulled in the entire constabulary to search for Stephen Fuller, had held a meeting earlier. Fuller, he said, had to be captured and soon. A town of nineteen thousand, the hub of this part of the state, just couldn't have such a man prowling its streets.

Anna, having finished her rounds as matron this morning— nothing noteworthy; just the usual sad assortment—glanced up from what she was reading and said, "What?"

"The book."

"Oh. I just ran over to the library and picked it up."

Peary, in a gray three-piece suit Anna hadn't seen before, went over to the coffeepot, poured himself a cup, and then came over and sat down with Anna. "Mind if I ask what you're reading?"

"Just a book on Goron."

"The one about his methods?"

"Ummmm."

"That's a very good book." He paused. "It was very nice seeing you last night."

She hesitated and then raised her eyes over the edge of the book. "It was nice seeing you, too."

"I hope—" He stopped himself. Smiled. Shyly. She'd never

seen him smile that way before—his vague air of arrogance gone—and she liked it.

"What do you hope, David?"

"Well, just that we—that we see start seeing each other more regularly."

She was neither coy nor cold. She said, quite matter-of-factly, "That's always a possibility."

He smiled again. This time it wasn't quite so engaging. It carried instead a certain disappointment and she was too nervous to endure his disappointment this morning. All she could think of was Stephen Fuller up there in the garage. Like a treed animal.

"Why are you reading Goron?" he asked.

Now she smiled. "Didn't the chief tell you?"

"Tell me what."

"I'm going to find out who murdered Parsons."

"But we know who murdered Parsons."

"No, we just *think* we know who murdered Parsons."

"But—"

"And I'll give you a hint."

"You don't need to give me a hint. I already know. It was Stephen Fuller."

"What if I said you were wrong?"

The old familiar smirk touched his lips. She would just start getting herself in the right frame of mind to really like David Peary, and then the smirk would come back.

He caught himself. "I don't mean to make fun."

"But that's what you're doing."

"Anna, he was in the alley with the murder weapon and—"

"What about the muddy footprints?"

"What do they have to do with anything?"

"And why, if he was really the killer, would he just stand over the body when he just as easily could have been running?"

"But he did run."

"Eventually—when he saw that everybody had already tried, convicted, and sentenced him."

David Peary sighed. "Anna, listen—"

She waved the small leatherbound book at him. "For all your talk about Goron and Bertillon, you sure don't take them very seriously."

"Not when we already know—"

She stood up. She had not slept well and for just a moment she felt a hint of vertigo. "All we know is that he was in the alley with the dead man and he happened to be holding the gun. That may sound a whole lot worse than it actually is."

"I really like that pinafore."

Obviously he was trying to make things gentler between them. She was going to snap off another rejoinder but she softened and said, "Thank you."

"You're just so darn pretty."

She laughed. "Yes, and especially this morning on about an hour's sleep."

"Want me to walk you upstairs to the jail?"

"I'm not going upstairs."

"You're not?"

"No, I'm going to ask some questions. I've got a day off coming because I worked two Saturdays ago, remember?"

"You mean you're going to start investigating—"

Before he could finish his sentence, she said, "You'll have to let me have a photograph of you in that hat with the lamp on it." Her laugh was tender rather than mean but he blushed anyway.

"I don't see what all you people find so amusing about my Ferguson."

"Is that what you call it? Your 'Ferguson'?"

He looked at her and he startled her by laughing. She'd never heard him laugh at himself before. It sounded wonderful. "I suppose I do look a bit ridiculous," he said. "But you can see very well, Anna. Very, very well."

She grinned at him. "I'll bet you can, David. I'll bet you can."

On her rounds that sunny morning, the packed-earth streets trembling with heavy wagon and trolley traffic, she saw many important citizens, each of whom had a pleasantry for her. It was one of those beautiful mornings when nice words bloomed, as did twirling parasols the color of cornflowers. There was W. B. Leach, judge of the superior court; Jasper L. Bever, cashier at City National Bank; William Greene, real estate owner; and a man named O. H. Hull whom the newspaper always described, somewhat vaguely and not without a certain note of bemusement, as "capitalist."

And there were farmers and railroad gang workers and mule skinners and shopgirls and gamblers and ministers and kids hanging onto their mothers. There was grass an eye-hurting green in Greene Square. There was shade black and sleek as silk beneath the awnings that fronted the businesses on First Avenue. There was silver breeze the scent of azaleas.

All this beauty, and most of it was wasted on Anna because she was so trapped in her determination to find out who was Parsons's murderer. She wheeled along on her Imperial with its colorful paint and genuine rubber tires.

Goron's method was very specific. The first people you talked to were those at the scene of the crime. Anna, who had a good memory, recalled every individual in the alley last night and spent the rest of the morning interviewing them. None offered anything new, just disappointment that Fuller had been allowed to escape, and the hint that his escape had been Anna's fault.

At noon she went over to Coffit's for a dish of ice cream and a cup of coffee.

Then it was back to her rounds, starting with the alley where Parsons had been discovered and where she'd noticed the muddy footprints. She knelt in the narrow, dusty alley and saw that crusted remnants of the curious footsteps remained.

Excited for the first time today, she began following the footsteps. She went down two blocks of alleys as dusty and yellow as the sunlight, the dark footprints clear as those left by some huge and ancient animal.

She had the thrilling sense that Chief Ryan and David Peary made far too much of this investigating business. All you had to do, really, was find some clue (just as Goron suggested) and follow it down and in no time at all you had your murderer.

Three blocks later the prints stopped.

Utterly.

The packed dirt alleys ended, replaced by a warehouse alley of wooden bricks.

She parked the Imperial and went over and got down on her hands and knees and began searching the wooden bricks. Working men stood on the docks watching her with eager and abiding interest.

She traveled the length of that alley on her hands and knees. She might have been scrubbing the blocks. But the footprints were gone. Entirely.

She went back to the section of dirt alley where they first began to fade and saw that the man had not taken the wooden bricks at all. He had veered left.

On the sidewalk she found the footprints again.

She went back and got her Imperial. She began tracking the footprints again, thinking that this investigation business was a lot easier than the men in the department liked to pretend.

She went four blocks on the sunny sidewalk, men still tipping their hats, women still fascinated by the shiny silver badge riding the breast of her starched blue pinafore, four blocks and—

The footprints ended.

Somewhat frantically, she leaned the Imperial against the steps of the Masonic library, and then began another intensive search—going east and then west; north and then south—in the surrounding blocks.

But nothing, nothing at all. The footprints had vanished once more. Utterly.

There was a man, a somewhat doughy man who everyone said was "tetched," meaning he'd been struck in the head by a baseball as a boy and would never again be quite the same, and it had fallen to him to become the sidewalk sweeper because his parents felt he needed something to occupy the years that turned his body into a graying man while his mind remained that of a child—even such a man as this needed work and so the city, at the parents' request, gave him a formidable wide broom and a gleaming galvanized steel trashcan on wheels and set him to work.

His name was Lem and, rather breathlessly, Anna rode up to him on her Imperial and said, "Good morning, Lem."

He grinned when he saw her. She was unfailingly nice to him and obviously he appreciated that.

"Lem, did you see any muddy footprints on the sidewalks this morning?"

She watched his face carefully. Sometimes even the most obvious concepts could prove elusive to Lem.

"Muddy footprints?" he said. He spoke with a kind of vocal clubfoot, the words dragging painfully from his mouth.

"You know. When you step in mud and then when you walk, you leave tracks."

His blue eyes—she'd always felt they were turned inward, witnessing some world no one else could ever understand, a dark world with which he'd made his peace—still registered nothing. And then abruptly she saw him smile. He pointed to his shoes. "Get bad stuff on your shoes?"

"That's right. Bad stuff. Have you seen any this morning?"

He nodded. "Over near Fifth Avenue. The 600s. Some bad stuff."

The street Lem described was only two blocks away. Easy enough to understand what might well have happened. The city had converted several avenues to wide brick lanes. If the man had left the sidewalk and walked up the street for a few blocks and then gotten back on the sidewalk—then his footprints would indeed reappear.

She touched him on the shoulder. "Thank you, Lem."

He pointed to his shoes again. "Bad stuff."

"Bad stuff," she agreed, and got back on her Imperial.

The tracks were there again. Clearly. Unmistakably.

She followed them three blocks down where they ended again at a short street that contained four very large and prosperous-looking houses, three of Victorian design, one a kind of stone monument that more resembled an institute than a home.

The prints went up to the edge of the grass and then disappeared once more.

Whomever they belonged to obviously had cut across the lawns here. Perhaps he'd gotten afraid and was running to find another alley.

She went around and looked in the narrow alley running behind the big houses. There were no footprints.

She went back to the sidewalk on the short street where the four imposing houses sat.

If the footprints went up to the grass but did not pick up again in the alley then that meant—

That meant that the killer may well have gone into one of the four houses in front of her.

Her first notion was that he might have forced his way in and was now holding a family hostage until he decided what to do. A similar incident had happened in Sioux City not long ago.

Then, as she stood leaning against her Imperial, an even scarier thought came to her.

What if the killer lived in one of these four houses?

How would Chief Ryan react when she said that she suspected one of the city's leading families of harboring a murderer?

Back on her Imperial, pedaling down the center of the street, she began to see how unlikely that particular proposition was.

Parsons's killer was no doubt of his own class—a homeless man with forged papers and a minister's garb that marked him as a confidence man, confidence men favoring such attire.

She decided, as Goron often said, that one of the best ways to know the identity of the killer was to know the true identity of the slain.

There were many more things she needed to learn about the dead Mr. Parsons.

TWENTY-THREE

"Do you remember him coming in?"

"Well, I guess I do."

"Rupert, this is important."

"Well, Anna, when you're sixty-eight your memory ain't always so sharp."

She smiled. "Rupert, you're as sharp as most of the people in this town and you know it. Who won the checker championship last year?"

"Maybe I just got lucky."

"Lucky. Sure."

Rupert put out a hand in which blue veins ran like pieces of rope and took the photograph.

They were standing in the Union Passenger Station over on Fourth Avenue and Fourth Street. With its steep roof and intriguing pointed tower, the depot's beauty had recently been praised by a writer from Chicago.

"Well," Rupert said. He wore sleeve garters and a green eyeshade. He had heavy wattles despite the fact that, though nearly six feet in height, he couldn't have weighed much more than a hundred pounds. He had sold tickets here since the railroad had come to Cedar Rapids.

He stared at the photograph. "Well," he said again. "He sure looks dead."

"He *is* dead, Rupert," Anna said patiently. "We always have murder victims photographed."

"Rank's going to have his hands full with this one." Rank was the west side undertaker and livery owner.

"So do you remember him?"

"Sort of, I guess."

She smiled. "You're some help, you are."

"I'm an old man."

"It would have been two days ago. When he came in."

"Two days ago."

"Yes."

Rupert snapped his fingers. "Hell's bells! Sure I remember him, and you know why?"

"Why?"

"Because he was the one who changed clothes."

"What?"

"In this here photygraph he don't have his collar on."

"Collar?"

"Cleric collar."

"He wore a minister's suit?"

"Yep. Least he did when he came out of the restroom." He nodded to a door across the broad depot that read GENTLE-MEN. The lobby was filled with a few dozen people sitting in long, comfortable, church-like pews, brightly colored carpet-bags at their feet. From the railyards nearby you could smell the almost sweet scent of train oil in hot sunlight.

"When he went in he wasn't a minister?"

"Right."

"But when he came out—"

"—he was a minister."

"I'll be darned."

"I thought it was kind of funny, too."

She said, "Thanks, Rupert. This has been very helpful."

He scratched a head covered with wisps of fine white hair. "You mind if I ask you a question?"

"Of course not."

"The chief give you a new job?"

She grinned. "Nope, Rupert, I'm doing this on my own time."

Rupert winked at her. "Well, I'd a lot rather have you asking me questions than that Peary." He shook his head. "You ever see him in that hat contraption he wears?"

Anna surprised herself by feeling small anger. "He's just doing his job, Rupert."

Then, to make up for the tone of voice she'd used with him, she patted his hand and left the depot.

Inside the constabulary, she went directly up to Szmeck, who was responsible for keeping all the physical evidence in neat little lockers on the first floor.

Seeing Anna, he said, "You wouldn't catch me hangin' around this place on my day off."

"I need a favor, Bob."

"Oh, heck."

"What?"

"I can tell by the way you're lookin' at me that it's a favor that's gonna get us both in trouble with the chief."

"No, it won't," Anna said reasonably enough, and then laughed softly. "Not if the chief doesn't find out about it."

The logical place to go after looking through Szmeck's locker of Parsons's belongings was to the hotel where Parsons had stayed.

Murchison, the desk clerk, a young man in a stiff collar, hair parted in the center, and blue eyes bright as gems, especially when they lit on a pretty lady, said, "You missed Detective Peary by twenty minutes."

"What?"

"He was here and asked me just the same questions you did."

"Oh."

"You never did have that spafizz with me."

"What?"

"One time I asked you about having a spafizz with me and you said you'd think about it. I'm on my lunch hour now. Why don't we slip across the street and have a couple of strawberry spafizzes and then we can talk."

She was irritated. What a cheap ploy to get a spafizz date with somebody. "I'm sorry but—"

"I'll tell you two things about Parsons I forgot to tell Peary."

Anna sighed. Did Goron or Bertillon ever have to put up with cheap passes made by hotel clerks with one gold tooth and wearing enough bay rum to make your eyes water?

Spafizzes were the most popular drink that year. They cost a nickel and you could get them in several fruit flavors. They were perfect for dates with young ladies who frowned on anyone who partook of alcohol.

They sat in a sunny corner in white chairs surrounded by young women in big colorful picture hats—blue, red, yellow, and green—and their beaux in cheviot suits and straw hats hanging off the backs of the chairs.

"So," Anna said, after they'd been served, "what about Parsons?"

"Why don't we just sit here and enjoy our spafizzes?" Murchison said.

Anna sighed.

Murchison apparently realized he needed to say something fast. He said, "You know how a spafizz is made?"

"Yes."

"With the fruit glooped down with a mixer?"

"Yes."

"And then carbonated water put in."

"Uh-huh."

"And then just a touch of cream?"

She sighed again. "I want to know about Parsons."

Now it was Murchison's turn to sigh. "The least you could do is be civil."

"I am being civil. I'm just not letting you manipulate me."

"There're a lot of women in this town who don't mind bein' manipulated by me at all. Not at all."

"Good. Let's go find a couple of them right now."

Murchison didn't laugh. "Anyway, since when are you a detective?"

"I'm a matron and on my day off the chief sometimes asks me to help out."

"Bullroar."

Anna said, "You were going to tell me about Parsons."

He sulked. He pouted. He stared out the window.

"Murchison," she said.

"Most women would be delighted to sit here with me."

Anna smiled. She'd never been impressed with people who had to keep telling you how impressive they were.

She said, "In thirty seconds I'm going to get up and walk out of here."

"I just wish you were nicer is all."

"We've been through that. Now what were you going to tell me that you didn't tell David?"

"You sweet on him?"

"Now why would I answer a question like that?"

"I just thought—"

"What about Parsons."

Trying to regain his balance—obviously Murchison *wasn't* used to being rebuffed the way Anna rebuffed him—he said, "I was just going to tell you about the telephone call he made."

"What telephone call?"

He squared himself slightly in the chair and warmed somewhat to his subject. "Well, you know how the telephone is right next to the office, just off the lobby?"

"Yes."

"Well, he made a call from there the afternoon he was killed."

"Do you know to whom?"

"No, but what's interesting is that when he came into the hotel he didn't look any too prosperous. Even when he wore that minister get-up, he looked kind of like a cheap drummer."

"I don't understand the point here."

"Well, that night, he stopped back in the hotel just when I was getting off. And he was a changed man."

How so?"

"For one thing, he was whistling."

"That's hardly a crime."

"But it was the way he was whistling. And the way he was carryin' himself, kind of a swagger like. And the new duds. Brand-new and darned expensive, too."

"I saw those."

"And," Murchison said with a certain note of triumph, "I

think this all had to do with the telephone call he made from the lobby."

"Why?"

"Think about it. In the afternoon the man's kind of a pauper and then all of a sudden he's whistling and got new clothes."

"Whistling and got new clothes," Anna repeated, running the concept back and forth across her mind.

"Whistling and got new clothes three hours after the phone call."

"Did you tell David this?"

"Not exactly."

"Why not exactly?"

"Because he didn't ask me. What he wanted to know was if Parsons had had an argument with anybody. Things like that."

She used her straw to get the last of her spafizz from the glass and said, "You wouldn't happen to know who he called, would you?"

"I wish I did."

"Why?"

He smiled with his gold tooth and his gem-like blue eyes. "Because if I did, I'd only tell you if you agreed to have dinner with me tonight."

She stood up, half-amused and half-irritated with him. "You're quite a man, Murchison, you know that?"

He decided not to acknowledge her sarcasm. Instead he pretended to take it as flattery. "So I've been told, Anna."

TWENTY-FOUR

He had once awakened in a horse trough drained of all but a half inch of filthy water. He had once awakened in a hotel room on fire because his cigarette had dropped down into the overstuffed armchair. He had awakened in a gutter in New Orleans. He had once awakened in the arms of a whore who had died sometime during the night of drugs mixed with raw moonshine. He had awakened in every humiliating, terrifying, disgusting, and loathsome way in which a man could awaken. And yet it had done no good for him, Stephen Wayne Fuller, no good at all, even though over the years he had tried every cure for drinking imaginable, from vegetable enemas, to medicines ordinarily given to llamas, to a Sioux Indian's "guaranteed" concoction that had raised snakebite-like blisters over Fuller's entire body and set him to vomiting until all that would come up was blood. So sick had he been that the only thing he could do when his legs were legs once more was totter down the dirt street to a tavern, where he got drunk as fast as possible so he could forget all the indignities the sly old Sioux had visited on him. (He would always later insist, Fuller would, that this was the Indian's way of making a single white man pay for all the villainies the settlers had set upon the red people.)

Now he awakened in a loft that smelled not of hay but of grease from the snappy phaeton wagon below.

He stood. He stretched. He spat. He rubbed his stubbled chin. He peed long and yellow in the corner. He smelled grass and he smelled sunlight and he smelled the sweet smell of the two-by-fours of which this garage was built. He eyed with some amusement a tiny calico kitten that sat staring at him with equal parts fascination and disdain.

The kitten was small enough to fit into the center of Fuller's hand. He brought the soft and warm little animal up to his face. It licked his chin with a pink, efficient tongue that smelled pleasantly of milk. Taking a store-bought cigarette from his shirt, Fuller took the calico and himself to a circle of sunlight on the rough loft floor. He sat there getting warm and watching the cigarette smoke, silver and blue in the light, and letting the calico sit in his lap and play with his string tie.

The hangover wasn't half as bad as the lapse of memory. That was always the worst.

Because anything could have happened and—

It came back in stark, undeniable images. Taking that first drink he'd sworn not to take and then entertaining God only knew how many people with his tales of Wyatt and Jesse and—

—and then the man throwing the drink in his face and calling him a liar—

—and then a gunshot in an alley and the young matron Anna hiding him here and—

The calico rolled over on its back (it was so young, Fuller wasn't sure if it was male or female) and started pawing at the silver-blue cigarette smoke. The quick, pink tongue was tucked for a rest in the corner of its mouth.

He petted its fluffy, white belly and then raised his eyes to a noise he imagined he'd heard at the opposite end of the ladder, where the ladder was.

"I've never shot a man before, but that doesn't mean I wouldn't," said a voice much too anxious to be saying this sort of thing at all.

One thing about hangovers. They always left Fuller irritable. So instead of being cowed by the huge Henry rifle the handsome young man was carrying, Fuller responded, "Why the hell don't you move a little closer so I can hear you?"

"This is as far as I need to come."

"You're law, I take it?"

"That's right. My name's David Peary and I'm a detective."

"I'll tell you something, Peary."

"What's that?"

"If I had to climb up a ladder carrying a big Henry like that one, I'd be afraid I'd drop the thing and accidentally shoot myself in the back."

He took some satisfaction from the fact that for just a moment—before Peary realized that Fuller's words were largely bluff—the detective turned at least a little bit pale.

"Another thing," Fuller said, and here he waved the calico that filled his fist, "I sure wouldn't want you to accidentally misfire and kill my little friend here."

"I'm arresting you for the murder of Mr. Parsons."

"I didn't kill him."

"There are a lot of people who say otherwise."

"There are a lot of people," Fuller said, "who still think that the earth is flat."

All the time he was talking, he was getting ready of course. There was a small hinged door that opened onto the slanting roof of a shed that stood next to the garage. What he was going to do was dive right through that door and then onto the roof of the shed and then he was going to roll off and start running down the alley as he had never run before.

There might be other lawmen about and those other lawmen might open fire but, given the case they had already built against him, it did not seem to matter much. Leave as not die in a sunny alley as dangle in front of a crowd a bit too eager for a glimpse of the dark journey that began at the end of a hangman's knot.

"You be careful of that Henry," Fuller said in a voice meant to irritate the young detective, and which obviously did exactly that.

Then Fuller set the calico down and put his plan in process.

With a yelp he dove through the door and then fell eight feet straight down to the flat shingled roof below.

About halfway down, his back began to hurt and he had to remind himself that he hadn't ought to be doing this sort of thing at his age. This was definitely the kind of stunt best left to younger men.

He hit the roof on his hands and knees and he heard an explosion from the small door above.

Then he tumbled to the packed dirt alley and started to scramble away, already out of breath.

This was *definitely* the kind of stunt best left to younger men.

TWENTY-FIVE

"Ten thousand dollars in cash, Susan Irene?"

"Yes, I'm afraid so."

Dunn, the banker, leaned back in his tall leather chair behind his wide mahogany desk in his big wood-paneled office with the stars-and-stripes draped on one side and the Iowa flag on the other and said, "This is most peculiar, don't you think?"

"Most peculiar, Larry? I find that an odd way to speak to someone who owns thirty-eight point nine percent of the stock in this bank."

"Still, Susan Irene." He paused. Lawrence Dunn was a chunky man in a dark suit, gold-rimmed glasses, and a spanking-bald, pink head. "I'm trying to be your friend."

"Then be my friend and give me the money I'm asking for."

"You know, the constables always tell us bankers to be alert."

"Alert?"

"Alert to people taking out large sums of money for seemingly no good reason."

"I'm hardly 'people.' "

His gray eyes rested gravely on her head. "I've never seen you wear a turban before."

"I wear it on special occasions. And this is a special occasion."

"Oh?"

"Yes—it's James's birthday."

"I see." There was that tone again. That tone that everyone in this town adopted whenever she mentioned James. There was scorn in that tone. There were sniggers in that tone. As usual when this happened, Susan Irene Eyles felt her heart flutter like a squirming animal within her chest in a kind of panic. For a judgment of James was, of course, a judgment on her.

Sitting here now, the room smelling of furniture polish and cigar smoke, she wondered if her first inclination hadn't been right. She'd originally planned to go to the vault and take out the major portion of her jewel and gem collection. This way, once on the continent, she could sell them and they could live comfortably for years, sending for her cash assets in Cedar Rapids a little at a time. She'd known that trying to withdraw so much cash was bound to attract nervous attention. But finally she'd decided that trying to sell the jewels and gems abroad might be too much trouble, and indeed prove danger-ous. Who knew what sort of villains might be dealing in such valuables? Or, just as bad, what if she were forced to take far less than their real worth? Then where would she be?

Thus far this morning she had been to the depot to buy tickets for tonight's 9:06 to Chicago (she'd wanted to leave today, but with everything to do that was impossible) and then to the pharmacist's for large supplies of her various med-icines (whenever the doctor told her there was nothing wrong with her, she simply went directly to the pharmacist herself and made her own case, something you could do when you owned the building in which the pharmacist worked). And then she'd gone to three different ladies' shops for piles of blouses, skirts, and undergarments—frustrating because she hadn't had time to judge these articles much by her rigid standards of fashion but was more or less forced to accept whatever they had in her large size. Finally, she had gone to two men's shops for James. Ordinarily, she liked his things to be tailor-made—everything from suits to shirts—but today she had to settle for rack clothes. She bought twenty-six pairs of socks because he was so rough on them, always wearing them out at the heel after only a few weeks or so. It was on her way out of the second men's store, the one where she'd bought twenty-six pairs of socks, and where the two male clerks had stood watching agape, that she realized she was probably being irrational. Couldn't she buy drugs for herself in Europe? Of course. Couldn't she buy clothes for herself in Europe? Of course. Couldn't she buy clothes for James in Europe?

"Is that a bandage?"

"I beg your pardon."

"A bandage. On your head. Under the turban."

The purple headpiece had slipped. She righted it quickly. "I bumped myself on the door."

"I see." But obviously he did not see; as his tone indicated, he did not see at all.

"I would like the money delivered to my house by four this afternoon."

"Are you going to be at our next board meeting, Susan?"

"Of course." She could see what he was doing of course. Trying to draw her plans from her. The reason why she needed ten thousand dollars in cash . . .

He leaned back in his chair, which squeaked of leather, and touched a gentle hand to his bald head. "I was a great admirer of your father."

"Thank you."

"And of your husband."

"I appreciate that."

"And though we've had our differences from time to time, Susan Irene, I am an admirer of yours."

She flushed faintly. She was concerned that the turban would slip again and reveal another flash of white bandage. "Thank you again."

"And that's why I'm probing so."

"Probing?"

"Asking you the obvious questions."

"What obvious questions? I don't know what you're talking about."

He leaned forward in his chair again. This time he folded his hands and put them on the desk. He had big-knuckled masculine hands. Comforting, purposeful hands that reminded her of her father's. But then that was Lawrence Dunn's demeanor—comforting and purposeful.

"Can't you trust me enough to tell me what's really going on?" Dunn said.

"I'm taking a brief—trip. That's all."

"A trip."

"Yes."

His eyes remained level on hers. "Do you mind if I ask where you're going on this trip?"

"Yes, Larry, I do mind. I mind very much."

He glanced at the turban once more. "The bandage is showing again."

"Well, it's hardly anything to be ashamed of. It's just a bandage."

"And you ran into a door?"

"Yes, James and I were moving some furniture and—"

"Ah, James, and how is he doing?"

"He's doing fine."

"James wasn't hurt?"

"Hurt?"

"When you were moving furniture?"

"No. He wasn't hurt. Just me."

"You may not remember, Susan Irene, but I grew up with James."

She felt great anxiety over his last remark without being quite sure why. "So you did."

"And I remember his temper."

"His temper?"

"I'm afraid we sort of—picked on him, I guess you'd say, and the older I get the more regret I feel over the sort of boy I was. I'm afraid I wasn't always nice to my playmates, maybe James in particular." His eyes addressed her turban again. "But sometimes James wasn't *easy* to be nice to. He'd get so angry—"

She once again adjusted the turban.

Larry Dunn said, "James did that to you, didn't he, Susan Irene?"

"Don't be absurd."

"He got angry and struck you."

"He'd never strike me." Now, helplessly, tears were in her throat and voice. "James is a good boy. He loves his mother."

Larry Dunn sat back in his chair. "You have a particular—situation—in your home. It's not your fault and it's not James's fault. It's just how life turns out. But sometimes in that—situation—well, sometimes, it leads to violence."

Blessed anger lacerated into action. She despised feeling helpless or depressed. Anger—pure rage—was much more tolerable.

She got to her feet as quickly as she could without knocking the turban off and said, "I don't know what you're getting at, Larry, and I don't care. But I would remind you of two things: I am not only a stockholder in this bank, I am also its largest depositor, and anytime I want any or all of my money, I have a perfect legal right to it."

He looked stunned by her wrath. "Believe it or not, Susan Irene, I was just trying to be your friend."

"I don't think it's possible for people with our different social backgrounds to ever be friends, Larry. I don't say that cruelly. I just say it as fact."

But of course she had said it cruelly and she could see in his gaze that she'd had the effect she'd wanted. Pain showed in his eyes. His father had been a bank clerk, a popular and trustworthy one to be sure, but a clerk and nothing more. Larry, Jr., had not even gone east to college but worked his way up by dint of sheer work and ingenuity to achieve his present position. Susan Irene would have preferred good lineage and social breeding.

Now Dunn allowed his own anger to show. "He hit you, didn't he, Susan Irene?"

"No." She felt on the defensive again and damned him for it.

"He needs to see a doctor, Susan Irene. He was in the bank a few months ago when one of our clerks made a mistake on his statement and he flew into an unbelievable rage."

"He's accustomed to having clerks do their jobs properly." She came down very hard on the word "clerks."

Dunn said, "You're going to take him away, aren't you?"

"As I said, that's none of your business."

Dunn's voice was friendly again. "I hope, for your sake, Susan Irene, that you find help for him. He could be very dangerous to you. Very dangerous." He nodded to her turban.

"My relationship with my son is none of your business. None of your business whatsoever." Her voice wasn't friendly at all.

He stared at her with what seemed to be part pity and part confusion. In a quiet voice, he said, "I'll have the money at your house by four o'clock."

"Very well," she said, and left without shaking his hand or any sort of goodbye greeting at all.

TWENTY-SIX

Fuller found the tracks seven minutes after tumbling from the flat garage roof to the alley.

The tracks smelled of creosote and the creek running blue nearby of clean water.

To the east were rambling hills of fir and pine and poplar. To the west were grassy bluffs on which lazed brown-and-white cows that seemed to be enjoying the purple buttons of clover and yellow buttons of dandelions that decorated the hills.

The tracks ran shining straight down the middle between east and west and Fuller ran straight along them, tripping every once in a while on an edge of tie or a particularly mean twist of dirt.

But he kept going.

He was too old and too scared to keep going, but there wasn't any other choice. With his hangover, and with the occasional thought of Boyd Haskell lying near-death in a small, white hospital room, not to mention the equally occasional thought of a kind and gentle-faced woman named Anna Tolan trying to help him, he did what he'd done all his life.

He ran.

He tripped, and his hands got bloody when he tripped, but he kept on running.

His lungs burned and his head, the hangover a disease, pounded but he kept on running anyway.

He started crying, thinking then of a jumble of things—of the woman he believed to be his mother there in the vestibule of the orphanage that night long ago; of the face of the mob in the alley last night when not one person showed any compassion or belief; of trying to accept what any man who'd spent his time gunfighting should have accepted long ago— that death, when it came, would come harshly, no family for comfort, no time for reflection—just the cold black oblivion of dying.

He ran as he had run all his life.

"You found him where?"

"In the garage at Mrs. Goldman's."

"Gosh."

"Why don't you sound more surprised?"

"I said 'Gosh.' Doesn't that sound surprised?"

"Not very."

"Oh."

"He was," Chief Ryan said, "in the loft of Mrs. Goldman's garage when a man with a white goatee—"

"That would be Mr. Tomlinson—"

"—when Mr. Tomlinson went out to the garage to relieve himself because he said that the 'women had taken over the indoor outhouse' as he calls it, and it was there he heard snoring and it was then that he climbed the ladder and saw a man he instantly recognized as Stephen Fuller sleeping off a hangover, at which point he forgot all about relieving himself and went in and picked up Mrs. Goldman's phone and called this department and we then dispatched Detective Peary."

"David?"

"David."

"And?"

"And what?" the chief asked.

"And what happened?"

"David leveled his Henry at him."

"Oh, my God."

"What are you getting so upset about?"

"And then what happened? He didn't shoot him, did he?"

"Who shoot who?"

"David didn't shoot Stephen, did he?"

"You call him Stephen?"

"Would you answer my question."

"No, dammit, David didn't shoot *Stephen.*"

"Stephen didn't shoot David, did he?"

The chief, lighting his pipe, shook his head. "No, David didn't shoot Stephen. Stephen being the outlaw he is, pitched himself through the loft door and got away."

"Oh—" She had started to say "Oh, thank God," but thought better of it.

The chief pointed to a chair. "I want you to go over there and close the door and then I want you to come back to this desk and sit down."

"You do?"

"Yes, I do."

"May I ask why?"

"You may but it won't do you any good."

She hesitated and then said, "Are you angry with me?"

"That's a fair assumption."

"But what's wrong?" She felt young, ridiculously and helplessly so, facing an inscrutable older brother or father. "What did I do?"

"I think," Chief Ryan said, and here he sounded more sad than angry, "that you did the worst thing a member of this department could do."

Already she felt her chest begin to constrict. Already she felt tears form in her eyes and her throat grow tight. "And just what would that be?"

"You helped a felon escape, Anna." He stared up at her and shook his head. "You helped a murderer escape."

TWENTY-SEVEN

He sat in his room as he had sat in his room all his life, on the edge of the bed with the French postcards on one side of him and a Nick Carter book next to him. Sometimes, especially on lazy summer afternoons when he lay in the sunlight shining through the window behind him, he would close his eyes and imagine that the postcards and the Nick Carter stories merged —and then suddenly he would not be fat, nor would his mother rule him, nor would the people in the town snicker when he walked down the street, nor would the people on his travels give him such suspicious looks when he simply tried to be courteous to them—no, then he would be Nick Carter, master of disguises, fighting crazed Apaches and evil spies who meant to use their futuristic inventions to take over the government of the United States—and the women in the post-cards would figure in these dreams too, needing rescuing from the Apaches and the evil spies, and he of course was only too glad to rescue them. He loved to close his eyes even tighter at this moment and imagine how the women would repay him for his daring. How they would swoon and thank him and—

He supposed that was why he didn't feel guilty about bury-ing Mother in the backyard. He hadn't meant anything per-sonal by it, he'd simply realized that this was going to be his one chance to escape her. He would go to Europe and start life afresh. He would be the man he'd always longed to be, the man she'd never let him be.

No, it had been nothing personal—

But then she'd reappeared last night and now . . .

Now, he heard her downstairs directing the two Mexican workers to be careful about loading all her suitcases and trunks aboard the wagon bound for the depot.

She hadn't even let him choose his own clothes.

She had come into his room early this morning, not even knocking really, just sort of rolling her knuckles across the door, and then pushing right in and shouting for him to get up and get dressed, that she'd just had a most disturbing talk with that lowlife Larry Dunn at the bank, and how surprised she was he hadn't gotten up very early to check on Mother and how she was doing following his unspeakable attempt to kill her (she still wore that ridiculous turban). Then she'd set about taking the things from the closet she deemed "proper," including the homburg she so much liked that he hated, and the white silk suit that some of the downtown loafers had greeted with particularly vicious catcalls the one day he'd worn it on the streets of Cedar Rapids. . . .

So now he sat in his room and thought about what he was going to do at nightfall.

He stood up and went to the window, feeling as always a fat and ridiculous figure even when alone—he had the terrible ability to see himself as others saw him, and to know in his pitiless heart that he deserved their ridicule—and looked down on the street at a smart new surrey clip-clopping down the street, at a young mother in gleaming white pushing a rattan baby carriage down the sidewalk, at a tiny blond boy with a gigantic red balloon that he kept jumping up in the air to reach, at a monarch butterfly flashing orange against the green of the new spring hedge. . . .

He would never be able to return to Cedar Rapids, and the odd thing—the thing he understood now for just the first time —was that he liked the city itself, found it beautiful and comfortable—

But, no, after tonight, there would be no returning. Ever.

He thought about the livery stable in the back and he thought about the pile of wood they stocked for the fieldstone fireplace downstairs.

Next to the pile of wood was a double-bitted axe that he remembered his father using to chop up firewood (his father had always said that chopping kept his muscles strong).

Now in his mind he saw the axe again—how both bits

glowed with a blinding white light, and how abruptly the blinding white light changed into dripping red blood.

Mother's blood, of course.

After she had finished crying, she told him everything, and then cried once again, and said, "But I still don't think he killed Parsons."

Chief Ryan sighed. "Anna, if I didn't half consider you my daughter, I'd order you out that door and tell you to never come back again."

She whispered, "I know you would."

The chief sat behind his desk and turned his pipe over and over in his big hands. "You had no right to hide him. You could make an aiding-abetting case, Anna." He looked stern."

"I know."

"And, frankly, I still find it hard to believe that you did it. You're such a sensible woman." He raised his eyes from his pipe. "When you spent time with him yesterday afternoon, you didn't—get romantically involved or anything, did you? I told you about his reputation."

She surprised them both. "Perhaps I did."

"Oh, God, Anna," he said.

"I don't know if 'romantic' is the right word," she said hastily, trying not to sound like a moonstruck young girl. "I thought he was going to be a stage actor sort—you know, the perfect profile and the deep speaking voice and all the suave nickelodeon business. But that isn't what makes him appealing at all."

"It isn't?"

"No. It's his—sadness, I guess." She shook her head. "He's lost—lost in his alcohol and lost in the fact that he was an orphan. I guess women just naturally want to mother him." She smiled sadly. "He really does need protection—from himself and everybody else, too."

The chief said, "I still have hopes for you and David. He's a very good man."

"I know he is."

"And anyway this Fuller—Anna, I'm not sure he's going to let us take him alive."

She did not cry or even sigh. She sat very straight in her chair and said in a flat voice, "I suppose that's true."

"He may even believe himself that he's innocent. A lot of drunks forget what they did and they go to the gallows swearing they didn't commit the crime."

"He didn't commit the crime."

"Anna—"

"I've made a list."

"A list?"

"That's why I told him to stay put in the garage while I worked through my list."

"Does this list have anything to do with what that French fellow—"

"—Goron—"

"—yes, that Goron—with what he teaches?"

"Yes."

"That's all I need." He put the pipe in the corner of his mouth. In the sunlight his white hair looked spun gold. "Anna, what we have here is a very simple case of murder. We've got motive, we've got proximity, and we've got witnesses. The county attorney always says he can win when he's got two of the three. We're giving him a home run."

"He didn't do it."

"The list?"

From inside her new pinafore—a light blue one—she took a piece of paper. "I'd like to read it to you."

"Right now there are twenty men and six dogs looking for your Mr. Fuller. Do you really think that reading this list is going to help anybody?"

"Would you at least listen."

"Damn," he said, "you sure can be stubborn."

She smiled. "And pardon your French."

"Very funny."

She consulted the list. "First there's the matter of the muddy footprints that I traced to a very short block that I believe the real killer lives on."

"Ah."

"And I believe it's because of somebody on that block that Parsons—who arrived in Cedar Rapids in very shabby condition and then pretended to be a minister—started swaggering and whistling."

"Swaggering and whistling?"

"That's what Murchison over at the hotel told me. He said that Parsons made a phone call from the lobby and then went somewhere for a few hours and then came back in brand new clothes, swaggering and whistling."

"You stay away from Murchison. You don't know what kind of man he is."

"I know exactly what kind of man he is, and that's exactly why I plan to stay away from him." She waved the list at the chief. "But I'm not done."

He sank back in his chair. "I know better than to try and stop you now."

"So what I plan to do is go to the phone company and try to find out who Parsons called. And then I plan to move in on the block where the footsteps ended."

"Those are pretty influential people there, Anna. You could get both of us in some real trouble."

But she went on, excited now. "And there's one more thing."

"What?"

"Would you expect a man like Parsons to have nearly ten thousand dollars in currency on him?"

"Not unless he'd robbed a bank in the last few hours."

"Well, he did."

"We didn't find any—"

Before the chief could finish speaking, she produced the plump white envelope she'd found on Parsons. She laid it carefully on the chief's desk. "I found this in his coat pocket."

The chief took the envelope and whistled as he counted through the money.

"Can you explain that?" she said.

"No. And I can't explain why you didn't turn this over before now."

"Because I didn't have the chance. I wanted to talk to you first about my list."

"Your list," he said, shaking his head. "By rights your list—"

"—should get me fired."

"Exactly."

She stood up. "I wish you'd light that thing."

"This?" He held up his pipe.

"Yes."

"Why?"

"Because the smell of it reminds me of my father."

He lit his pipe with a lucifer and sat back and she leaned forward on the edge of his desk.

"I know you're going to keep hunting Fuller down," she said.

"That's right, Anna. I still believe he's our killer."

"But I hope you'll let me work through my list."

"I can't make you a detective, if that's what you mean."

"No, but you can give me the rest of the day to ask my questions."

"A lot of citizens are going to complain about a woman playing detective."

She laughed. "That's where you're confused."

"Confused?"

She waved her list at him. "I'm not *playing* at all, Chief. I'm very serious." She started out of the chief's office then stopped herself and inhaled deeply the pipe smoke. "Boy, that smells great, it really does."

Then, before he could raise any more objections, she was gone.

TWENTY-EIGHT

In certain ways they had always disgusted David Peary, the bloodhounds. They salivated too much and they rutted too often and their dewlaps were ugly and their sad inscrutable eyes put him off. And they were not half as dependable as popular opinion seemed to hold.

But there was the odd occasion—such as when they'd tracked the escaped convict all the way from the prison in Anamosa up through the surrounding bluffs and then all the way over to the Cedar River—that the dogs had indeed been dependable, owing largely, he supposed, to their history. Bloodhounds had been in favor long before Christ, in the countries around the Mediterranean Sea and by now had been bred into admirable if not infallible animals. . . .

But there was still the smell and slobber of them and—

"He's been spotted, sir!" came a cry from behind Peary who, along with two blue-uniformed constables, had been letting the dogs lead them along the railroad tracks near Bertram crossing.

Peary turned and watched a third uniformed constable make his way up the steep rocky grade, below which ran the blue river.

"Spotted where?"

"In a barn near the railyard."

"And who spotted him?" Peary did not mean to sound cynical but he knew that most "sightings" proved to be nothing more than frustrating and wasteful detours from actually catching the culprit.

"A farmer, sir. Leading a cow to town."

Peary frowned. "You really think they're on the scent?" he said to one of the two constables who'd been guiding the dogs.

"Sure am."

"And you don't have any doubt about it?"

"Not a bit."

He had to make a decision and make it quickly. "I'm going to put you in charge, Riley," he said to the panting constable who'd just come up the grade with the news.

"Me?" Riley said, sounding astonished.

"Right."

"But aren't you—?"

"I'm going to gamble on the dogs and stay with them."

"But the sighting—"

Peary said, "I'm going to have to take the chance that the sighting is wrong." He put his hand on Riley's shoulder. "It's going to be up to you, Riley. Entirely up to you—if he's actually in that barn."

Half an hour later, with three Cedar Rapids constables shouting for the man to come out of the barn with his hands up, Riley said, "Damn. Look."

"It's Gramps McHune."

Gramps McHune was a local hobo who slept in a different barn every night. At Thanksgiving a family always had him in for dinner and at Christmas the nuns always gave him, in addition to food, a present or two.

"Damn," Riley said again.

He'd hoped to prove David Peary wrong and capture Stephen Fuller all by himself, thereby making Peary look foolish at the least. Riley, on principle, did not like men who wore suits and ties.

As he came toward them with his hands up and his britches falling down, Gramps McHune was snapping his wooden dentures into place.

"Damn," Riley said again.

Exhausted, Fuller pulled himself up into the boxcar and lay on his back, panting the way he had seen heat-stressed cows pant when they were near death in the scorching sun.

The car smelled of wood and grease and human excrement. Obviously hoboes had used it recently.

Presently the car was on a siding about two or three miles east of Cedar Rapids. At least that's how far Fuller estimated he'd come.

He lay there trying to puzzle through what had happened and what lay ahead. He had no gun, little money. And he needed very badly to go west where he could lose himself somewhere in the last vestiges of the frontier.

He wondered how long he could stay in this boxcar. . . .

The dogs were leading the constables up through a stand of pines that led to a rock ledge along which ran railroad tracks. The undergrowth was a tangle of thistle and burr. At first Peary tried to keep picking the burrs from his suit pants but finally he gave up and just let the things ride on his worsteds like leeches.

By now he had lost what faith he'd had in the dogs. If they had indeed scented Fuller, then the gunman was far ahead of them.

One other thing troubled Peary and that was the inevitable talk there would be back in town about him holding a Henry on Fuller—and Fuller getting away. There would be a great deal of smirky conversation about Peary's academic criminology credentials and his fondness for military demeanor within department ranks and a great deal of smirky conversation about how Anna Tolan seemed smitten by Stephen Fuller.

Burrs clinging to him, he pressed on down the railroad tracks. Ahead, there were three boxcars on a siding. . . .

Fuller snapped straight up the moment he heard what, as an ex-lawman, he knew to be the sound of his own doom.

Bloodhounds.

Instinctively, he reached for a weapon that wasn't there. Sweat covered his face and back. His heart raced and a sour taste rose from his stomach.

He edged up to the sliding door and peered out.

There were three constables, including the one who'd

nearly captured him in the garage, and they were being dragged along behind three very healthy-looking hounds.

He took a deep breath, trying to prepare himself for the physical cost of another hard run, and then got himself ready to jump out of the door and head straight up the bluff before him. . . .

"The dogs are on to something, sir."

"How can you tell?"

"Look at them salivate."

"You can tell from that?"

"That's one way, sir." The uniformed constable said all this with just the faintest air of amusement, just not enough that he could get reprimanded for. "I'd say the boxcars, sir."

Peary, raising his Henry, said, "You wait here with the dogs. Both of you."

"But, sir—"

Peary knew that the only way he would overcome the mistake he'd made in the garage this morning would be to take Fuller single-handedly. Then there would be no doubt about the detective's competence. Not even in the detective's own mind. . . .

Two hundred yards ahead three red steel boxcars belonging to the Chicago and Northwestern sat vivid against the blue sky and green rolling bluffs. Near the roadbed squatted two sleek black ravens and a red squirrel, watching Peary as if he were putting on some kind of show for them.

"You're sure you don't want some help, sir?" said the first constable. He was only citing procedure, which called for the car to be surrounded.

"We'd be more than happy to—" began the second.

Peary, a bit dramatically, patted his Henry, adjusted the same hat on which last night had rested the Ferguson Univeral Reflecting Lamp, and then said, "This time our Mr. Fuller won't give me any trouble at all. No trouble at all." He wanted to say *If your dogs are right for once and he's even in there* but he knew how important morale was to constables and he did not want to endanger their abiding faith in the hounds.

He prepared himself. . . .

Fuller jumped as far and wide as he could, hitting the edge of the knee-high prairie grass that swept all the way up to the crest of the bluff.

A stab of pain in his left ankle caused him to begin limping. He knew immediately that he'd suffered a sprain, perhaps a bad one.

Having refused the aid of his two officers, Peary had moved down the tracks, tiptoeing so his feet would not make undue noise on the rock bed. He drew within five feet of the second boxcar when Fuller came bursting out.

The Henry seemed to discharge of its own volition, the blue spring air thunderous with noise and tart with gunpowder.

The recoil of the three shots jerked Peary back several feet.

Not a single shot hit Fuller as he limped his way up the bluffs.

"Should we let the dogs have at him, sir?"

But before Peary could speak, the dogs made up their own minds, snapping free of the constables' hands and bounding on Peary who was, after all, in their way.

The hounds knocked Peary flat to the ground, his Henry firing one last ineffectual time.

Then they took off chasing the gunman up the hill.

By now, Fuller was clutching his leg as if he'd been shot. The pain in his ankle was that bad.

But he did not stop moving as quickly as he could. He had smelled something promising—water—and he knew that his only hope was to reach the crest of the bluff before the hounds, now unseen but loud in the deep, waving prairie grasses reached him.

Below, near the boxcar, the three constables had gathered themselves for another go at him and were discharging round after round, and the dogs were deafeningly loud, seeming to be nearly right next to him now.

Dragging his foot, Fuller came out of the grasses to a small clearing next to a stand of white birch. He moved a few more feet down the opposite side of the bluff and there he saw it, the river.

There was no time to think or make plans. The drop was maybe thirty feet. Perhaps there would be a swift and pitiless current that would drown him. But at this point it did not matter that much—

The clamor of gunfire and the slavering dogs were upon him now—

—and he jumped.

His stomach twisted much as it had this morning when he'd leapt from the loft door. His entire body anticipated how hard the impact with the water would be from this distance.

The last thing he heard before he broke the blue water was the disappointed yapping of the hounds.

TWENTY-NINE

"I'd appreciate it if you could look."

"You never did bring me that rhubarb pie recipe you promised," Colleen O'Dwyer said.

"Darn," Anna Tolan said. "I forgot that, didn't I?"

"I suppose you're just so busy being a detective and all." Colleen smiled and then giggled. "You're a strange one, you are, Anna Tolan. Half the men in this town wantin' to marry you and—"

"I'd say half is a bit of an exaggeration."

Colleen O'Dwyer sat at the switchboard in the offices of the Iowa Telephone and Telegraph Company. She was a thin, pretty woman of forty-two with her gray-streaked auburn hair pulled up in a loose chignon. She wore a prim, high-collared blue dress that complemented perfectly her merry, blue eyes. She was Anna's best friend.

"George brought another one around," Colleen said.

"Colleen—"

"A cravat salesman. Very nice looking but a little on the dull side. I said he wasn't good enough for you and—"

"Colleen, I really am here on official business."

"Oh, official business. Soon I'll be lucky if you speak to me at all."

"Please, Colleen, don't you have some way of finding out where the calls were placed from the hotel the day before yesterday in the afternoon?"

But relentless Colleen could not quite be stopped. Not yet. "Personally, I think you should give David Peary a bit more of a chance. He's a little stuffy, I'll grant you, but he has the makings of a good husband." She sighed and said. "My George has his pompous side, too, Lord knows but—"

"Colleen, please." In addition to trying to get her remarried, Colleen also spent much of her time talking about how lucky she'd been to find a man of her husband George's caliber, which, in fact, Anna agreed with. George was a fine man.

"Excuse me a second," Colleen said. The switchboard had *burred* softly. She rearranged her headset (which looked very futuristic and seemed filled with the promise of the millennium that would be coming up not many years from now; daily there were stories of contraptions that almost successfully raised up in the air and flew . . .) and said, "Good afternoon. May I help you. The post office? You might jot down, Tessie, that that's line number 18. For future reference, I mean." She patched the appropriate line into the appropriate slot on the switchboard and then made note of the call on a long tablet, then sat back and said, "It'll be easier than you think, Anna. We keep records."

Anna said, "I guess it was worth hearing your whole marriage spiel after all."

"I'll be done here in five minutes and then I'll take you back and we can look through the log. How's that?"

"Worth enduring an evening with a cravat salesman."

Colleen laughed. "Why don't I invite you and David Peary over for cards some night."

Anna said, nodding to the big Ingraham clock on the wall, "Four more minutes and we can go look at those logs."

"Look," Colleen said, "here's a call that afternoon from the hotel to number 523." Then she paused. "Just a minute."

The back room of the phone company was piled high with boxes containing new telephones. What had been a novelty only a few years ago was rapidly becoming a necessity, the $1.50 monthly charge moving other things out of the family budget to make room for the new invention.

Colleen reached over and picked up a long sheet that had been published by the *Evening Republican* that listed all Cedar Rapids and its neighbor Marion phone numbers. "523 would be in the block where you found the footprints."

"It would?" She could not keep the excitement from her voice.

"Yes. The—" Colleen ran her finger down the long sheet of newspaper. "The Eyleses."

"The Eyleses," Anna said to herself, trying to picture the family.

"He ran the shoe company."

"Oh." But the picture was still not clear.

"And she's that very fancy lady who's always giving teas to show off all the things she bought in Europe. There are a lot of write-ups in the paper about her."

But there were two or three such women, Anna thought. And—

"And she has that odd son that she can't let go of even though he's in his forties. James."

And then of course it was very clear.

You saw them everywhere, mother and son. Anna had always felt sorry for the man, sensing his humiliation in being trapped in his public and peculiar relationship.

"The Eyleses," Anna said.

"Yes," Colleen said. "Isn't that odd?"

THIRTY

Late in the afternoon, he went out to the shed where his father had once cut wood and he picked up the axe and he held the long handle, tracing its curving length with plump fingers, smelling the damp earth of the shed floor and the straw odor of the nest a robin had built just under the door, and then his fingers fell to the double-bitted axe itself.

He had once watched his father cut the head off a Thanksgiving turkey. He had cried when he'd seen the animal's head fall like a stone to the earthen floor, and the blood bloom in a perfect circle, and his father had looked at him in disgust, and said, "You'll always be your mother's boy, James. Always."

Now, all these long years later, holding the same axe in his hand, James stood in the shed dizzy with so many feelings he could not sort them out—fear and love, loathing and esteem, loneliness and the great giddy prospect of happiness, real happiness, at last.

He wondered how mother's head would look falling off so silly and horrible, just the way the turkey's falling head had looked. He wondered if the blood would bloom in so perfect a circle.

He took the axe and left the shed and went back inside the house.

When she saw him, she knew that something terrible had happened, and her first image was of Stephen Fuller lying dead.

He sat alone on a long bench outside the chief's office. He sat doing something she'd never seen him do before—smoking a cigarette. He sat with his head down with what were obviously the traces of tears in his eyes.

She could not help herself, unprofessional as she suspected she was being.

She went over and sat next to him. She did not say a word because she knew it was best to just sit next to him and offer reassurance simply through her presence. Always before he had been so arrogant in so fragile a way—she knew why he was a laughingstock among the more hardened constables—but now that arrogance was gone and she felt for the very first time something like pleasure in his company, even though she still feared that Stephen Fuller might well be dead.

The chief came out after a time, pipe in mouth, papers in hand, starting off down the hall in the opposite direction. But when he saw them he paused. He started to speak and come over but she shook her head. Understanding, he nodded and went about his business.

Through a barred window came sunlight and in the sunlight were dust motes of a quality peculiar to late afternoon. Overhead the floor groaned and squeaked, the prisoners being led down the back stairs for their exercise period. Blue uniforms appeared now and then and grim gazes fell on him and she began to realize that it was not Fuller to whom something had happened but rather to the man she sat next to, David Peary.

After a long and painful time, he spoke in a voice that showed he was half of himself. "I let him get away, Anna. Twice now."

"Twice?"

"We had him trapped in a boxcar but I wouldn't let the men help me and—" He shook his head miserably. "And he got away."

"I'm sorry, David."

"I've told the chief I'm going to resign."

"Oh, David."

"It's only right."

"It isn't right at all. You're a good detective. You really are."

He glanced over at her and smiled. "Yes, I saw last night

how much respect you had for me in my Ferguson Reflecting Lamp."

She grinned back. "I didn't say you were a perfect detective, David. I said you were good."

"I still don't know why everybody finds my Ferguson so laughable. It comes in handy."

"It's just ahead of its time and everybody laughs about things that are ahead of their time."

"Do you really mean that?"

"Yes."

"You're really a friend, Anna."

She reached over and took his hand. "This is a terrible thing to say, David, but you've never been more likeable to me than right now."

"Than right now? I just let a killer get away—twice."

Gently, she said, "He isn't a killer."

"Oh, Anna—"

"Listen, David, how would you like to help me find the real killer. I think I'm closing in."

"Anna, I really appreciate—"

"Now you're being the old David. Arrogant, closed-minded—"

He sighed and folded his hands in his lap and looked straight ahead at the wall. Finally, he said, "You really think you know who killed Parsons?"

"Yes."

"Who?"

"Do you know the Eyles family?"

"The Eyleses? Anna, she's a pillar of—"

"Are you willing to listen to some things with an open mind?"

"Of course, but—"

"Don't say 'of course' like that unless you mean it. Now, are you willing to listen?"

He paused. "Yes."

"Good."

So she told him.

Obviously he was careful in responding to sound as if he'd

not only listened attentively, but weighed what she'd said seriously. "Footprints?"

"Footprints."

"And just what would they prove?"

"That someone from the Eyles house went from there to the alley where Parsons was killed. I followed the tracks."

"And the phone call. What would that prove?"

"That Parsons called somebody in the Eyles household."

"Meaning?"

"Meaning that the Eyleses are very wealthy and meaning that they would be one of the few people who could give him ten thousand dollars."

"The money you found in his suit coat?"

"Exactly."

"But why would they give him ten thousand dollars?"

"That's what I've been thinking about and I'm afraid there's only one conclusion."

"And that is?"

"That is that Parsons knew something about one of them—most likely James Eyles—and that they paid him the money to keep quiet."

"But what did he know?"

"That's why we've got to get into the Eyles house."

And then he realized what she was proposing and he said, "Oh, Anna—Oh, Anna."

"David, listen—"

"I'm in so much trouble already and—"

"Over Stephen Fuller?"

"Right."

"Well, before we go to the Eyleses we're going to find Stephen Fuller."

"We are?"

"Yes."

"But how?"

"We're going to ask a friend of his where Stephen might be inclined to hide out."

David Peary said, "This isn't a good time to ask, I know,

but Anna when you talk about Fuller you—you get kind of excited. You're not—"

"—no, David, I'm not." She touched his hand again. "I feel sorry for him. He's a very sad man and right now he doesn't have many friends at all. I want to help him and catch the real killer and I want you to help me." She smiled. "Tonight, you can even wear your Ferguson."

Then she leaned over and kissed him on the cheek. Behind them they heard the squeak of leather oxfords, the squawk a big man makes.

The chief said, "Do you really think that's how you should conduct yourself in a constabulary—especially with a killer on the loose?"

Anna, airily, stood up and said, "You don't have to worry about your killer, Chief. We'll be bringing him in sometime tonight."

And with that, she and David left the station, the chief saying behind them, "I'm not going to accept your resignation, David."

Anna said, "Good. Because he's withdrawing it, anyway."

With that they went down the stairs and out into the late afternoon sunlight.

THIRTY-ONE

He slept. He sweated and he rolled back and forth on the bed and sometimes he dreamed of his father and sometimes he dreamed of the imaginary French woman he had invented years ago and sometimes he dreamed of the cellar and what it was like to take a tiny mouse in his big hands and—

The knock woke him.

He woke, sweat covered and disoriented, and listened as, far off, downstairs, he heard the knock and then heard his mother speaking with somebody and then heard the door shut and steps fading into the sounds of the street.

The money.

His mother had told him that somebody from the bank would be delivering a great deal of cash in time for the train that would be departing tonight at 9:06 for Chicago and from there to New York and the steamship.

He staggered up from his slumber, feeling almost drunk, and then went down the hall to the bathroom and washed his face with clean, warm water from the basin. He washed his neck and under his arms and then he washed goop from the corners of his eyes and then he splashed on a nice-smelling cologne and then went back to his room where he put on a fresh shirt with a fresh celluloid collar and fresh pressed pants and then he went over to the corner where the axe stood and he raised the axe and looked at it, just looked at it, and then he went out of the room and down the stairs.

She was in the living room, sitting on the blue brocaded divan, and he came up behind her and he knew that he couldn't afford to give her any sort of chance at all because she'd speak to him and make him feel guilty and then he wouldn't be able to do anything at all.

So he did the first part of it quickly, using the back of the axe as a club, a single swift blow to the crown of her head.

She slumped over. There was almost no blood. He walked around to the front of the brocaded divan, careful not to step on the edge of the Persian rug that she was always saying he tracked on with his feet.

She was very heavy. When he lifted her he started to career backwards, like a vaudevillian at the Greene Opera House. Then he began to career forward. He could not seem to quite find his feet. He was sweating and it was exactly the sort of sticky sweat he hated so much (one of the men he'd killed—Ohio, perhaps—he'd been in 103-degree temperature . . . and cleansing away the glue-like feeling of his own sweat had taken days).

Finally, with her cradled properly in his arms, he began his walk out the back door to the cellar. From his right hand dangled the axe.

The day had been warm enough that the basement smelled quite damp. Curiously, he liked the smell. It had a peculiar sweetness to it. He supposed he thought of it as a "safe" smell. While the cellar was for the most part his prison, at least he was safe down here. No laughing eyes or whispers. No bullying from Mother.

As he laid her down on the floor, she moaned. He could not recall any sound that had ever infuriated him more.

The woman was indestructible.

He cracked her once more with the flat end of the axe, this time near the temple. She did not groan again.

He took her hands and dragged her over by the rows of preserves and jams where there was a drainage indentation in the packed dirt floor. He arranged her neck so that it fit exactly on the lip of the indentation.

When he moved back to get his axe, he turned abruptly and caught his face in a silver spider's web. He sneezed and cursed. He knew he would have a rash. Any kind of contact always gave him a rash. He wondered what kind of salve Mother always put on him to get rid of the rash. Well, he'd just have to pack all her little round tins of salves. One of them was bound to work.

He had raised the axe and was just about to set to work when he heard the knocking upstairs.

He looked down at Mother, perfectly laid out and all ready, and knew that he dare not do it now.

She might scream at the last moment and be heard.

No, he thought, he'd have to go upstairs and find out who was knocking.

He was almost in tears.

"Doesn't seem to be anybody here," David Peary said.

"Let's give it a few more minutes."

Peary said, "You really think this is a good idea?"

"This is the house Parsons called that afternoon from the hotel."

Peary glanced up at the stained glass door and all the leaded windows in the fine big house. "It's just that the Eyleses are such an old and respected family and—"

In the dusk of birdsong and lilacs, in the dusk of jays and the distant silver laughter of children playing, they both heard the same sound at the same time.

Footsteps.

Heavy footsteps.

Coming to the door.

"Hello?" he said.

Anna recognized him at once of course. James Eyles. In his dark suit and clean shirt and cravat, he looked quite impressive. If he hadn't been so fat, he would have been a handsome man.

"Hello," she said.

"May I help you?"

He didn't seem to recognize either of them.

David Peary showed his identification. "We're with the Cedar Rapids Constabulary."

"Oh."

"And," Anna said, "we were wondering if we could ask you a few questions."

"Questions?"

"Are you familiar with the Parsons killing the other night?"

"I heard about it, I suppose."

"Well, we're investigating it."

"I see."

Anna hesitated. "Did you know Parsons?"

"The dead man?"

"Yes."

"No."

"He telephoned here the afternoon of his death."

"He did?"

"Yes."

James Eyles snapped his finger. "Oh, that's right. I forgot."

"I beg your pardon."

"Mother's rug."

"Her rug?"

"She has a very rare Persian rug and he telephoned to see if he might stop over and see it."

"Parsons was interested in rugs?"

"So he said."

"You don't sound as if you believed him," Anna said.

"Frankly, I didn't."

"You didn't?" Peary said.

"No. Frankly, I thought he was just using an excuse so he could get inside the house."

Peary said, "For what purpose, Mr. Eyles?"

"Well, so he could come back later and rob us. Mother is very trusting and I'm afraid that sometimes she lets people use her."

"Is your mother home?" Anna said.

For just a moment, Anna sensed an uneasiness in Eyles. "Yes. But she's resting."

"I don't suppose you could ask her to talk to us?" Peary said.

"She has a very bad cold and really needs her rest, I'm afraid."

Anna said, "Do you mind if we look around your yard?"

"Our yard?"

"Yes."

"Why would you want to look around our yard?"

"Just procedure, is all. We're trying to match Parsons's footprints with certain prints we found in the alley where he was killed."

For the second time in the conversation, Anna could hear James Eyles's tone become strained and high-pitched. "That seems a very odd request."

"We're just doing our job, Mr. Eyles," David Peary said.

Obviously seeing that he had no choice, Eyles said, "All right. But I'd like to accompany you."

"You would?" Anna said.

"Yes?"

"Do you mind my asking why?"

"Not at all. Mother has so many things planted. I just want to make sure you don't step on anything." He paused and for the first time smiled.

For a reason she could neither understand nor explain, James Eyles's smile chilled her.

"Do you have any objection?" he said.

"No," Anna said. "No objection at all."

So they set out walking around the yard, looking for the source of the muddy footprints the other night.

All James Eyles could do as they walked around to the side of the house was clench his fists and hope that down there in the cellar, her head just waiting to be severed from her shoulders, Mother did not wake up and cry out.

"Careful," he said to the female constable to whom he'd already taken a profound dislike. "You almost stepped on Mother's azalea."

Then he saw where Anna Tolan was looking.

Right at the cellar door.

THIRTY-TWO

In his orphanage days, Stephen Fuller had once stolen a piece of candy from the grocery store where all the kids hung around and shot marbles and saw who could pull their red licorice into the longest strips. He had taken the candy on a dare, when Mr. Flannery was in the back of the store, and the moment he slipped the piece of chocolate into his pocket, he heard the creak of Mr. Flannery's shoe leather and then the guilty giggle of the children who had dared him—and then he knew he would be caught.

That was how he discovered the bluffs on the west side of the river, and the rock promontory that looked out over the blue span of water to the rocky fir-covered heights rising from the opposite shore. In those long ago days, escaping to the bluffs had given Fuller the security of penetrating the deepest forest where nobody could ever find him, where things remained shade-dark and shade-cool despite the intense yellow heat of the sun.

After fleeing the bloodhounds and jumping into the river, he let himself be carried downstream with the current, taking care to stay to the side of the river so that he would be less easy to see, and ducking under the water for as long as his lungs could stand. He thought of the drunken woman who'd come to the orphanage and demanded to see him. He should have been thinking about the police. He should have been thinking about who really killed Parsons. He should have been thinking about how he was going to get out of Cedar Rapids. Instead he thought about the woman and the longer he thought about her, the more clearly he understood *why* he was thinking about her. Because soon now he was going to join her. . . .

Dusk took the day just as Fuller came out of the river and scrambled over the sand and dirt shore to the grassy incline leading to the bluffs above and the ragged rock promontory.

By now he no longer noticed pain—the way his lungs burned, or head pounded, or the way his knee bled from a cut he couldn't recall inflicting. He did not notice the birds or the faint early fireflies. He did not notice the sweet, reedy smell of the river grass or the sweet birth smell of the spring mud. He did not notice the imposition of stars on the night sky or the lean racing dog angling rightward from the western edge of the bluffs—

There was just the sound of the drunken woman in his ears—

—and his relentless and ceaseless running . . .

The man tripped him. It was that easy. Fuller did not even see the man until it was far too late.

The man wore a gray fedora and carried a fat double-gauge and wore a three-pointed star that said he was with the constable's auxiliary. He had white hair, and a big friendly Irish nose and he looked like just the sort of man any right-thinking boy would want for a grandpa.

"I don't want to have to shoot you, all right?"

Stephen Fuller heard this from his sprawled position in the river grass. He tried to say that he wasn't going to do anything, but he couldn't. His lungs and his throat and his head hurt too much.

The man moved back a few steps. In the dusk light his fedora was the brightest thing on the landscape. His double-gauge smelled of gun oil and the man himself of pipe tobacco. He said, "There are forty men looking for you."

"I know."

"You'll be a lot safer in jail."

"I guess so."

"You won't give me any trouble?"

"No." He paused, there on the ground, there in that moment that he knew was one of the last of life as he'd known it. He got on his hands and knees like an animal. The cut knee hurt badly. He said, "You know something, mister?"

"What?"

"I didn't kill that man." His voice sounded so young there in the dying day. Young in a crazy way, high-pitched and pleading. "I really didn't."

"You get up easy now, all right?"

"Did you hear me?"

"I heard you. Did you hear me?"

"So you don't care that I didn't kill him?"

"I'm just part of the auxiliary constables. I'm not no judge. You didn't kill him, I'm sure you'll get a chance to tell your story." He moved the double-gauge right in line with Fuller's face. "Now you get up easy, all right?"

"All right."

"You're lucky it was me."

"Why's that?"

"Because some of the auxiliaries, they're scared of you. Likely to be heavily armed and very nervous. Which wouldn't be a real good combination for you."

He thought of having a go at the man. He had enough raw energy, and certainly enough fear, to make such a move. He wasn't even afraid. It was just that he didn't want to run again. Ever.

He said, "Can we walk along the river instead of taking the road back?"

"Why's that?"

"Maybe there'll be a dance at the pavilion. We'll be able to see the lights and hear the music."

"You're a damn curious one, I'll say that for you." Then he shrugged. "Guess it doesn't matter much to me."

Twenty minutes later, he was in a jail cell and Chief Ryan was offering him a cup of coffee and saying he'd better have that knee looked at.

Chief Ryan didn't seem in the least angry. He wasn't like frontier law. He was intelligent and civilized, even considerate. He was a professional. He asked if Fuller felt like talking and Fuller said no, he was sorry, but that at least for right now he didn't feel like talking at all. Chief Ryan said okay, that he'd send a doc up to check the knee and then they could talk.

It was early in the evening and all the cells were empty except the one holding Fuller, so he had nothing holding him back anymore. He could do exactly what he wanted to. He sat on the edge of the cell, looking up at the glimpse of starry night sky from his dark cell window, and he thought once more of the sounds the drunken woman had made that night demanding to see him—grief and rage and self-pity—and he thought of that useless and ceaseless encumbrance called his life, and all the ways he had managed to make a muck and a mess of it, with the alcohol especially, and he knew exactly what to do then, what prisoners in jails that Fuller himself had run would sometimes do.

In the starry darkness, the jail floor throbbing with the business of constables below, the cell itself smelling of the beaten men who'd been here before him, Fuller began tearing the pillow case into lengthwise strips and then knotting them together. They would be strong enough and the window would be high enough that there would be the snap. He would not just dangle. There would be the quick and blessed snap. . . .

He worked on, quickly and deftly. He would not have much time. . . .

THIRTY-THREE

"Did you see how he looked every time I went near the cellar?" Anna asked as she and David Peary hurried back to the station.

"He's hiding something. There's no doubt about it."

"We should have gone down there. Why did you stop me?"

In the soft light from the street lamps, David frowned, looking both purposeful and boyish. The fonder she'd grown of David, the more she noticed that about him—how all of a sudden he could look like a little boy, despite all his efforts to seem in control. He sighed. "I'm ashamed to say it, Anna, but it's just politics."

"Politics?" she said, steering the Imperial down the sandy street. "What's politics got to do with it?"

"Not Democratic or Republican politics. Social politics."

"Oh. In other words, rich versus poor."

"Unfortunately, yes. His mother's a very powerful woman. If we'd just pushed past him and gone down to the cellar, we could have gotten the chief into a lot of trouble." He adjusted his derby.

Anna, watching him, said, "Would you ever let me pick out a hat for you?"

"Huh?"

"Your hat. You should wear a different kind of hat. That's an old man's hat and you're not an old man yet."

He glanced at her quite reasonably, as they waited for three buggies apparently headed for the Greene Opera House to pass, and then said, "I've tried other kinds of hats but they don't work."

"Don't fit you mean?"

"No, don't work. Aren't able to support my Ferguson Universal Reflecting Lamp."

"I see," Anna said.

He had never looked nor sounded more like a kid.

"But you don't have any proof?" Chief Ryan asked.

"No, and we won't have any till you let us go down there," Anna said.

They were in the chief's office. There was an air of celebration in the station owing to how easily Stephen Fuller had been apprehended. Auxiliary constables lounged in the front of the station talking with regular constables. There was a lot of laughter and the cigar smoke smelled as rich and fine as the spring night itself.

Some of the smoke made its way into the chief's office where it mingled with the chief's own haze of pipe smoke.

"The footprints led right to his house," Anna said. "You've got the wrong man upstairs. I just know it, Chief. I really do."

The chief frowned. "You sure picked a good family to bother."

"Goron says that sometimes you need to deceive your suspect."

"How do you do that?"

"Simple," David Peary said, taking over now. "We go back to the Eyleses' and tell James Eyles that we think that Stephen Fuller hid out in his cellar on the night of the murder and that we need to search the place for any clues."

"So he thinks you're trying to back up the Fuller matter?"

"Exactly."

"Well—"

"He won't suspect, Chief. He really won't," Anna said.

Chief Ryan bit on the end of his pipe. "His mother could make things damn tough for me." He started to say "pardon my French" but Anna waved it off.

The chief was about to say more when the shouting started

upstairs. Heavy footsteps came down the creaking stairs leading to the chief's office. A constable who looked pale and confused came through the chief's door without any sort of announcement at all.

"I cut him down, Chief, but I'm not sure he's alive."

"What?" Chief Ryan said, sitting up.

"Fuller," the officer said. "He hung himself."

Less than a minute later, Anna knelt beside the prone form of Stephen Fuller. The officers had rested him carefully on the cell bunk. One of them had run down the street for a doc.

They got his collar open and they propped his head up on a pillow and they kept checking for a pulse. His throat was so bruised it almost appeared to be a knife wound.

He looks dead, Anna thought. He looks very old and dead. She thought this with a mixture of depression and dread. She liked Stephen Fuller; not because of the charm the chief had warned her about but because she sensed that he was a decent man caught up in situations he could not control.

And she believed absolutely that he'd had nothing to do with the murder of Parsons in the alley.

"Poor fellow," David Peary said.

Anna was surprised and moved by his tone of real sympathy.

The doc, a squat white-haired man with a cigar and a black leather case and a wart on his nose, came up the stairs two at a time.

He said nothing to nobody, simply made his way through the group and into the cell.

He said, "How long ago was he cut down?"

"Maybe ten minutes."

The doc nodded, started checking Fuller's vitals by putting his head to the unconscious man's chest.

Anna, scared, said, "Is he all right?"

The doc seemed irritated that she'd asked any sort of question at all. "Now how am I going to find that out, young lady, if you keep interrupting me?"

He went back to his work.

THIRTY-FOUR

Her head came off with a single fall of the axe.

He watched, fascinated, as it rolled away from the body and went into the small depression in the cellar floor. The turban rolled away to the other side.

Then it stopped rolling and James went over and turned it right side up so that it stared at him with all the summary malice Mother had always been capable of.

As he stood in the cellar that had so long been his prison, as the hand lantern spread an almost friendly glow through the gloomy confines of this dank tomb, he felt for the first time since the days of his father a real freedom, marred only by the lingering glances of the two constables who had been here.

It had been all he could do to keep them from the cellar. It was as if they'd somehow known that Mother was down there.

He felt burdened again, then smothered by the very years of his existence—of his weight, of the derision that had been the constant of his time, of the useless and boyish dreams that even he knew were foolish for a grown man to hold. It was then, standing there with massive clenched hands, that he began to cry, though of course the tears were not for Mother or for what he'd done—but were rather for himself because he understood in some final way now that he himself was his own prison, that some pitiless fate had made him so, that even with Mother's head severed, and even with the prospect of Europe before him—he would always be doomed to being himself.

A shudder moved through him as he squeezed the last of the tears from himself. He became, abruptly, cold, both physically and spiritually. He saw what needed to be done and prepared to do it.

Those two detectives—the slightly apologetic man, the

pretty young woman far too brazen for his own taste in women—would be back—and soon.

He had to move immediately and quickly. The train would be departing in twenty-five minutes.

He went over and knelt next to mother's head. He reached across and plucked up the turban and set it on her head, covering the bandage she'd so skillfully fitted herself with.

Then he leaned over and kissed her once on the cheek. "Goodbye, Mother," he said.

Then he set to business.

THIRTY-FIVE

"Is it on straight?"

"Let's see," Anna said, holding up her thumb to appraise the angle at which David's Ferguson Universal Reflecting Lamp sat on his derby. They stood on the sidewalk before the massive Eyles home. Fireflies cut through the air like divers showing off in a swimming pool. Nearby rosebushes lent the air an exhilarating sweetness. Past the quarter moon trailed lacy gray clouds. "It needs to go a little more to the left."

"The left."

"Right."

"There."

"Looks very nice, David."

"You want to laugh, don't you?"

Anna sighed. "Right now, there's not much to laugh about, David."

"The Ferguson's going to come in darn handy when we go down into the cellar."

"I know it will, David."

He put his hand on her arm. "There's something I should say."

"What?"

"You don't need to go in there with me."

"What?"

"You don't need to go in there with me. We're—not sure what we're going to find."

Anna said, "Well, thanks a lot."

"I was only being a gentleman."

"No, you weren't David. You were being a prig. 'Women-should-stay-home-and-knit-doilies.' That's what you really meant."

"No, I—" Then he stopped himself. He looked tall and handsome there in the shadows. With his Ferguson glowing he also looked like a very young boy again, too. "I'm sorry."

"You're sorry?" She'd never heard David apologize before. Ever.

"Yes. I shouldn't have said that at all. I was just being a prig and I apologize."

"Gosh, David."

"What?"

"I'd lean over and give you a kiss but I'm afraid I'd knock your Ferguson off."

"Evening, Mr. Eyles."

"Evening." James Eyles handed over his ticket to the conductor. The train was issuing dragon-like steam from its innards and inside the yellow windows he could see ladies in big floral hats and men in handlebar mustaches and children drugged with sleep now that it was getting later in the evening. In one aisle two men stood smoking cigars and nearly bumping portly bellies and laughing about something they found terribly funny. In the dining car a very beautiful young woman held a glass of sherry aloft and then sipped it with her sensual lips. James Eyles felt the same air of festivity he did whenever he boarded trains. Anything could happen on them and you could meet anybody. Anybody.

"Business trip?" the conductor said, as Eyles stepped up to the train proper.

James Eyles glanced at the man and smiled. "No," he said. "Pleasure. Pure pleasure."

"Well," the conductor chuckled, "have yourself a good time."

Once they got him breathing regularly, they moved him out of the small white room tart with the smell of antiseptics and moved him down the hall to the room where one of the nurses remembered his earlier visit this afternoon.

The nurse and the doc who'd taken care of him brought him into the room, waking Boyd Haskell in the process.

Haskell, groggy, asked, "Is that Stephen Fuller?"

"Yes."

"What happened?" Boyd Haskell asked.

The doc told him.

"My God," Boyd Haskell said. "My God."

In the moonlit darkness, they stretched him out on the bed and then put blankets over him and then left the room.

A uniformed constable stood guard just outside the door. Cradled in his arms was a ten-gauge.

"My God," Boyd Haskell said.

The cellar door creaked open. With it came odors pleasing as preserves and fetid as mildew and damp aged earth never allowed sunlight.

"You ready?"

"I'm ready," Anna said. "You ready?"

"I'm ready. I was just checking to see if you were ready."

So they went down the stairs that pitched to the right and that were somewhat slimy with moisture. David, because he wore the Ferguson, went first. He had his Colt out and at the ready.

Anna sensed something wrong, oppressively so. She was having a little trouble breathing and hoped that David was good with his Colt. Very good.

He slipped on the last step. He shouted two curse words so blue they surprised Anna. She wouldn't have imagined David saying such words.

She saw his fall, how his arms splayed out, how from the back of him he appeared to jump off a cliff, then she saw nothing because when he hit the cellar floor his Ferguson went out.

"Are you all right, David?"

Nothing.

"David?"

"I'm embarrassed, Anna. That's how I am. Embarrassed."

"Well, it wasn't your fault. These stairs are slippery is all."

"This will make a good story back at the station."

"Well, nobody back at the station's going to know about it if you don't tell them."

In the gloom, his voice softened. "Really?"

"Really."

"Gee, Anna—"

She sensed he was going to get romantic again, even sprawled there on the cellar floor, and while she felt a similar inclination, she fought it. "Do you have a lucifer?"

"Yes."

"Well, let's get your Ferguson going and take a look around."

"Good idea."

He got to his feet, wiping off as much of the muddy dirt as possible, and then Anna came down the rest of the stairs, her shoes making squishing sounds as she groped her way across the cellar to David. "There's our mud."

"What?"

"The footprints from the other night. Feel the floor."

"Gosh, you're right."

"Let's get that lucifer going. If Eyles or his mother are upstairs, they're bound to have heard us by now."

He handed her the lucifer. "It's usually easier if I sort of squinch down and somebody else lights the Ferguson."

Anna smiled at his choice of words. "All right, you 'squinch' down and give me the lucifer."

It took three lucifers, actually. Two to find where the ignition hole was and one to light it.

In such close quarters, the Ferguson threw off startling illumination, yellow light revealing a coal bin, wooden shelves filled with rows of glassed preserves, and a corner piled high with newspapers that ran back several years.

The first thing Anna wanted to check was the color and texture of the mud. She thought of a case Goron had worked on, a very similar case, so she knelt down and rubbed the mud between her fingers next to the Ferguson. "See. The same kind of red clay base. We've got our case, David. We really do."

Then she saw how, at the end of the coal bin, the cellar took an abrupt right. "Why don't we check back there just to be sure."

"I'm just surprised they haven't heard us by now."

"So am I, actually."

David shrugged. "Well, let's give it a look."

They went around the corner and David said, very quietly, "Anna, I'm going to give you your choice."

He put a strong, gripping hand on her arm so that she could not move.

"What's wrong, David?" She knew it must be terrible because his face was pale and sweaty and his eyes had a certain crazed glaze over them.

"Why don't you just go and get the chief, Anna?"

"David, I'm a part of this case, too, don't forget."

"Anna, I'm just trying to do you a favor."

But she pushed his arm off and squeezed past him there in the narrow aisle leading to the back of the cellar and there, thanks to the light of the Ferguson, she saw it.

Her Catholic school training was sufficient that the first thing she did was cross herself and say "Jesus, Mary, and Joseph." The second thing she said was, "He killed his own mother." She took David's hand and led him, little boy-like, into the back corner of the cellar.

"There's the axe," she pointed out. "The county attorney will definitely want that." Then her brave and efficient tone dimmed and she said, nodding to the severed head across from them in the flickering light, "Do you get the feeling she's watching us?"

"Yes."

"You scared?"

"Kind of. You?"

"Kind of, too."

David said, "We should both take real deep breaths."

"Really?"

"Yes, I was reading a magazine article about that just the other day. How that helps."

So they took real deep breaths, Anna with her eyes closed. When she opened them she saw a severed head, its neck ragged and bloody, and the torso of what had once been a woman on the edge of a slight depression in the dirt floor.

She shook her head. "I don't think it helped all that much. Do you?"

"No," David said. "I'm afraid it didn't."

"Why don't we go upstairs and see if he's there. If he's not we can call the station."

"Great idea."

Neither of them needed to tell the other how badly they wanted out of the cellar.

Eyles sat in the bar car and ordered a whiskey sour. He loved whiskey sours. He spoke briefly with a drummer from the Baltimore area and even more briefly with a very handsome woman from Chicago. He realized, watching her, that not until tonight had he ever killed a woman before, and then it had to be his own mother. The drummer from Baltimore came back after making his way around the bar car with a joke about a priest and a rabbi, and then Eyles and he started in on another conversation, this about the gold standard and the general incompetence in Washington. It was obvious that the drummer, slightly drunk, knew nothing about politics but Eyles was grateful for the company. He kept glancing at his pocket watch. He just wished the train would pull out.

"Anything upstairs?"

"No," Anna said, coming back down the broad stairs. For a moment, she wondered what it would be like to live in a house this splendid, the chandelier probably costing as much as the tiny house Anna had grown up in—or more.

"I found one thing," David said, sounding quite proud of himself.

"What?"

"A note by the telephone. One or both of them had train reservations for tonight."

"The 9:06?"

"Right."

"Gosh," Anna said. "He'll be leaving—"

"Right now!"

Anna thought a moment. "I'm going to get on my handlebars and you're going to get us to the station. All right?"

"I'm sure going to give it a try," David said, adjusting his Ferguson.

THIRTY-SIX

The drummer from Baltimore was telling Eyles a joke about two fat people amorously attached.

Eyles, knowing it was the height of rudeness, interrupted the drummer as a conductor walked by.

"Excuse me, sir," Eyles said, always polite just as Mother had taught him to be, "but shouldn't we be leaving soon?"

"A few minutes I'd say."

"But we're late." A whine had come into his voice.

"Only by twenty minutes, sir." The conductor winked. "That's only a venial sin. It's not a mortal sin till it goes past an hour."

With that, the black-uniformed man moved on out of the bar car.

"So anyway these two fatties . . ." the drummer from Baltimore continued.

Eyles had begun to sweat and shake.

"Boy, you're heavier than I thought," David said.

"Thanks a lot."

"You know what I mean."

"No, I don't happen to know what you mean."

"It's just that you're so little and trim. I just expected this to be like giving a child a ride."

They were on First Avenue now. Wagons and buggies rolled by. Anna knew now that they should have called the station for help. She was up on the handlebars and then suddenly she jumped down.

"What're you doing?" David said.

"You pedal the Imperial," she said. "I'm going to run alongside."

The drummer from Baltimore said, "There's two ladies over there alone."

"Over where?"

"In the corner."

"Oh." But James was becoming so overwrought, he could scarcely see. The bar car was packed now, its gilt trim and short mahogany bar and tiny tables beautiful and melancholy in the soft lamp glow. The air was hazy with smoke and perfume and the excited words of travelers. The scene looked like an illustration out of a magazine.

The trouble was, he wouldn't be able to appreciate any of it till the train began to move.

Then he heard the magic word from the platform outside and he felt a relief so profound he nearly collapsed.

" 'Board!" shouted the conductor from the platform outside.

They reached the train station sweating and breathless, David having caught his cuff in the bicycle chain, Anna having tripped once and scuffed the palms of her hands.

The train, a huge metal monster, all splashing light and smoking fury, was still in the depot.

"Look in the train windows!" Anna said. "You take the east end, I'll take the west."

By now the train wheels had begun their slow but inexorable churning and as Anna's feet slapped along the wooden platform and she peered inside the golden windows, she realized that in only moments the train would be running five and then ten miles per hour.

She thought of telling David to jump aboard but he was lost in the milling crowd of well-wishers come to wave goodbye to loved ones and relatives.

She had no choice but to jump up the two metal steps and enter the train proper. She thought of the severed head back in the cellar and shuddered. She wished she had David's Colt.

The train was packed. Kids cried and old men coughed and young women hummed to infants. Conductors with formidable bellies glanced at Illinois railroad watches and drunkards snored loud as buzz saws.

"Excuse me," she said to a conductor. "I'm looking for a man."

"Husband?"

"Hardly. I'm with the department."

He stared out at her from his jowly face and said, *"You're* with the constables?"

She went through four conductors before she found one who recognized the man she was talking about. He said, "Bar car."

David Peary was standing with his Ferguson Universal Reflecting Lamp still intact though no longer lit and his eyes desperately searching each car as it whipped by him in the night. The cars were a yellow blur, like moving streaks of yellow paint dappled here and there with the brown of a tweed coat or the auburn highlights of a woman's hair.

Eyes searching the platform, trying to find Anna through the thinning crowd of wavers and well-wishers, he felt a curious dread, as if something terrible had just taken place but he didn't know what.

It was just then that he turned back to look at the panorama of the passenger cars as they left the station—and saw Anna.

She was working her way down the narrow aisle of a sleeper toward the rear end of the train.

"Anna!"

He began shouting at her, though above the clamor of the train, any human noise was irrelevant. He waved at her, though she was so intent on her destination that she did not see him.

"Anna!"

Now David began running along the platform, watching as the caboose came into view, with the brakeman standing on it smoking his corncob and waving at the people on the platform.

"Anna!"

James was getting up to find the men's room when he saw her.

At first he thought he must be confused, that it could not possibly be the young female constable who'd come to his home, and had looked at such length and so curiously at the cellar door.

He continued to stare, assuming that as she pushed further into the bar car, she would suddenly lose her resemblance to the young woman—Anna Tolan her name was—but the opposite took place. The closer she got, the more she resembled Anna.

James ducked down—the drummer from Baltimore in the middle of yet another joke—and began his passage out the rear door of the bar car.

Anna saw the back of his head just as he opened the door and started out.

She wished more fervently than ever that she had David's Colt. One of the older constables had taught her, two summers ago, how to shoot, and she had great confidence in her abilities.

"Excuse me" she said and "excuse me" and "excuse me," pressing through laughing men and giggling women, following James Eyles's bald pate the way her brother had always taught her to follow a flyball when it was arcing high in the sky and about to drop down. *Take your eye off it for even a second, Anna, and you'll lose it,* William had always told her somberly.

His bald pate went out through the door.

"What the heck kind of contraption is that?" asked the brakeman who'd taken David Peary's hand and pulled him aboard.

"The Ferguson?"

"It's called a Ferguson?"

"Yes."

Even when the thing wasn't lit, it attracted attention.

"I'm afraid I don't have time to talk," David Peary said, showing the brakeman his badge. "I'm looking for a woman."

The brakeman shrugged. "Aren't we all?"

James had no idea where he was going. Just toward the rear.

He knew she was still following him.

Anna had no idea where James Eyles was leading her. Toward the rear of the train, most likely.

She wondered if he would risk jumping off, now that the train had gathered speed.

She hoped not. She would not want to jump off after him.

David Peary had no idea where he was going. Just toward the front of the train.

He opened the door leading to the next car and stepped across the open passage that smelled of train oil and heat and the cold rushing night. He got a nice glimpse of the starry sky and then he opened the door leading to the next car.

And then he saw James Eyles.

And then he saw Anna.

"David!" she shouted. "Stop him!"

Before he had time to get his Colt out, James Eyles hit him with a fist that felt like a falling brick.

David Peary was so stunned, he crumpled to the floor, feeling his Ferguson Universal Reflecting Lamp fall off in the process.

Anna jumped over David on the way to the door through which James Eyles had just gone.

She got her hand on the knob and pulled it open. Given the opposing force created by the speed of the train, this was no easy matter.

But she pried the door wide enough to slip through.

Which was when Eyles's hands found her throat and lifted her up and slammed her back against the door that had just closed.

He meant to kill her.

She had never had occasion to know anybody who actually meant to kill another human being before—so not only was there the physical pain of being banged back into the door, there was the shock of seeing another human being so enraged.

She kicked, she clawed, she tried to scream. Nothing did any good.

She cursed, she prayed, she let spittle fly from her mouth and smear over his face.

She caught glimpses of the night sky, wan quarter moon, drifting gray clouds, and through the sweat of him and the fear that filled her she had the sense that she was smelling the last odors of her life—that soon breath and then existence itself would rush from her.

Abruptly, she fell backward, through the door she'd come from, and to the floor, Eyles still on top of her and choking her. David had opened the door from the other side and she got a glance of him standing above with his Colt.

Then, enormous even above the clatter of wheels and the roar of the engine, she heard the sharp *crack* of the Colt— once, twice, three times.

Eyles's hands loosened, and he fell back finally, staggering to his feet, face streaming with blood, a look of disbelief in his eyes.

He got to the door before David fired again, getting him in the neck this time, and then Eyles spun out of the door and over the railing of the train.

He screamed all the way down and when he hit the gravel roadbed, you could hear a terrible cracking and crunching of bone.

They stood there, the train hurtling cold and metallic through the night, watching the dark and bloody form recede.

"Oh, God," she said, "Oh, God."

She fell into David's arms.

THIRTY-SEVEN

The nurse said, "He can't talk. The rope really cut into his neck."

It was midnight. Anna and David had been at the station explaining everything to the chief. A crew had gone along the tracks and found Eyles's body.

Now they were at the hospital. Anna wanted to be the one who gave Stephen Fuller the news.

The nurse didn't turn on a light. She did not want to wake Boyd Haskell. She asked Anna if she would whisper. Anna nodded then followed her into the room.

He lay, very old and curiously frail looking, in a white bed that seemed to swathe him entirely. Only his beard stubble, black in the moonlight, gave any hint of the virility that had made his reputation.

He was awake. She could see his eyes there in the darkness. They shone with a misery she could scarcely stand to watch.

She said, "We found the man who killed Parsons."

It took him a while but finally he brought his gaze over at her. He nodded.

"You're free," she said.

He made a sound that was like a bitter laugh.

"You could always stay here," she said. "In Cedar Rapids." She nodded to the bed in the opposite corner. "You could stay on to see how Boyd does."

She sensed his rage. His inability to speak probably made it all the worse.

"The chief said to convey his apologies."

He had gone to staring off again, not looking at her.

She said, "You're a decent man, Stephen. You really are. Maybe once you get your life in order you'll find out that things don't have to be so bad for you all the time."

He did not look at her.

"Well," she said, and there were tears in her voice and she damned herself for them, "I've said what I came to say anyway."

And with that she turned and left the room.

Or started to, anyway, before he grabbed her wrist with the deftness of a striking animal and brought her close to the bed.

In a voice that was as if a wound were talking, he said, "I appreciate what you've done for me."

Then he let her go.

She began to say something else but then she realized that there was nothing else *to* say to a man as complex and unto himself as Stephen Fuller.

She was just about through the door when he rasped out one more sentence. "You should marry that Peary guy, Anna."

In the darkness she could see the most unlikely thing of all, Stephen Fuller smiling.

She rode the Imperial and David Peary walked along beside her. It was chill enough tonight that there was silver frost on the green grass and smoke coming from chimneys.

David was lamenting the condition of his Ferguson. "I'll

just have to buy another one," he said, pointing to the lamp that had been crushed during his scuffle with Eyles.

Anna thought how much things had changed in two days, when she'd been laughing at his Ferguson. Now she said, "I wonder if Goron ever wears a Ferguson."

"You know, Anna," David Peary said, in that quite-serious tone only he seemed capable of. "I've wondered that myself."

And then, not sure why, just happy about things in general, she laughed and said, "I'll bet you have wondered about that, haven't you, David? That's just the sort of thing you *would* wonder about."

Then she stopped the Imperial and drew him to her and kissed him there on First Avenue, not so far from the rushing Cedar, not so far from the trolley tracks, not so far from the soda shop—and not so far from where she planned to spend the rest of her life.

Then they went the rest of the way back to Mrs. Goldman's among the lonely cry of dogs and the sweet scent of apple blossoms on the chilly spring night.

ABOUT THE AUTHOR

Edward Gorman is the author of several novels in the western, mystery, and horror genres. He is editor of *Mystery Scene* magazine. His most recent Double D Western was *Graves' Retreat*.